PRAISE FOR *TH*

'Fleshing out the shadowy ____ novels, this intellectual romp is the best debut I have read in years.'

NICHOLAS LEZARD, *The Guardian*

'The staff of the office are revealed as gatekeepers to the after-life, setting up a neat reversal in which determining the resting place of recently departed souls is treated like any normal job – employees rock up late and use work computers for their own projects – while mundane tasks, such as making couscous salad, are addressed with scholastic intensity.'

SAM KITCHENER, *The Literary Review*

PRAISE FOR *RECONCILIATION*

'Absent, slippery or suspect 'facts' are central to this unapolo-getically knotty novel.'

STEPHANIE CROSS, *Daily Mail*

'This ingenious novel succeeds in being both a highly readable story of second world war derring-do and its aftermath and a clever Celtic knot of a puzzle about writing itself.'

JANE HOUSHAM, *The Guardian*

'Moving between various real-life events, each laced with errors and lies, Ware demonstrates to the reader how easily we can be misled as he explores the ethics of storytelling in this wartime thriller.'

ANTONIA CHARLESWORTH, *Big Issue North*

PRAISE FOR *THE FACULTY OF INDIFFERENCE*

'*The Faculty of Indifference* is both funny, diverting, exhausting and baffling all at once. Whatever your tastes, Guy Ware is a writer whose name should be part of the contemporary literary discussion. His is a post-modernism that pushes the past into our increasingly confusing world.'

REBEKAH LATTIN-RAWSTRONE, *Byte the Book*

'Ordinary life is a terrifying prospect in this existential satire about a London spook . . . *The Faculty of Indifference* is a book of dark shadows and dry humour. It's a comedy about torture, death and loneliness, and an existential drama about a world that swirls and twists and turns on us without provocation.'

JAMES SMART, *The Guardian*

GUY WARE is a critically acclaimed novelist and short story writer. His stories have been listed for numerous awards, including the London Short Story Prize, which he won in 2018. *The Guardian* described *The Fat of Fed Beasts* as "Brilliant . . . the best debut novel I have read in years." Guy was born in Northampton, grew up in the Fens and lives in southeast London.

GUY WARE

THE PECKHAM EXPERIMENT

CROMER

PUBLISHED BY SALT PUBLISHING 2022

2 4 6 8 10 9 7 5 3

Copyright © Guy Ware 2022

First published in Great Britain in 2022 by
Salt Publishing Ltd
12 Norwich Road, Cromer, Norfolk NR27 0AX United Kingdom

www.saltpublishing.com

Salt Publishing Limited Reg. No. 5293401

A CIP catalogue record for this book is available from the British Library

ISBN 978 1 78463 263 2 (Paperback edition)
ISBN 978 1 78463 264 9 (Electronic edition)

Typeset in Neacademia by Salt Publishing

Printed and bound in Great Britain by Clays Ltd, Elcograf S.p.A

For Sophy

And for my former colleagues inside the Castle

"If a man's character is to be abused, say what you will,
there's nobody like a relative to do the business."
Thackeray, *Vanity Fair*

7th–8th of June, 2017

DIANA FUSSES AROUND behind me, plumping cushions on the sofa for no good reason, because these days I don't make too much of a dent. She's come to talk me out of it, I know she has, but I'm playing dumb. I don't want her thinking I've any fewer marbles than I have, so I said earlier, when she arrived, Diana, darling, I said, when she let herself into the flat with the key she's insisted I give her, just in case - she doesn't say in case of what, but we both know - It's always a pleasure, I said - *lied* - and she said: For me, too, Uncle Charlie, look, I've brought you some kitchen roll, and I thought: kitchen roll? What was the woman up to? But: Truly, I said, perhaps a little too quietly for her to hear, the wonders of the Orient, I said. Which was from a nativity we did here, at the Pioneer Centre, the old Peckham Experiment, when we were kids and you were Joseph - *Joseph, for Christ's sake* - and it stuck in the family, the way things do, and

~KIT - CHEN - ROLL!

Diana shouts because she likes to pretend I'm deaf, or hard of hearing, she says. But: I'm not deaf, I say, just a little . . . overwhelmed, by your generosity. She says: You didn't have any last time, remember? When you spilled your tea? We both know it was gin, not tea: can she not bring herself to say the word? - *Unless it was brandy? Not gin?* - It was not tea, anyway, although it was possible I had it in a teacup, I do that sometimes, so as not to offend her sensibilities. I say: Do you know what projection means? And she says, Speaking clearly? EEE-NUN-SEE-A-SHUN? Like the actors do? ~Very funny, I say. It means seeing your own subconscious fears and failings in another person, specifically, your analyst. And she says: Well, you'd know all about that, wouldn't you? And really, what is she? Eight? – *don't say really* – she doesn't mean it, she knows I've never been in analysis, it's not something the working classes do, or wasn't, anyway, so what she means is: I've read books, I know big words. She means I always was a bit above myself, which can't be a good thing, can it? So I say, You brought me kitchen roll, in case I spill my gin again and haven't been shopping? What she's trying to forget is that I've got my own slippers, my own teeth and – best of all – my own front door, even if she has a key as well, and okay, I have my own mobility scooter, too, but you can't have everything, and I get around –

you do

– I do, which is the Beach Boys, like you didn't know, 1964, all summer long, and so what if you were already too old for pop? Or what we called old, then, what we called pop, then, when we had no idea. So what if you were in your 30s? Because I was, too remember? 'I Get Around'?

you always did

that's right, I always did

All Summer Long was the LP

like you didn't know.

I turn away from the table I use as a desk and wave the page at Diana. It's all I've written up so far. She asks me what it is and I say: My script. For tomorrow. She says, It's not a play. I say: Would you rather I . . . what's the word? And anyway it is a play: I'm acting, I know exactly what the word is. I'm old, not gaga. ~What word, Uncle Charlie? ~The word I want. Would you rather I . . . ~Prayed? ~Good God, no. Don't be stupid. Would you rather I . . . *extemporized?* Her face is pleasingly blank, and I'm pretty sure it's horror, not incomprehension, which is what I'm after. She is picturing it. The risk. Given the choice, she'd rather I said nothing at all. She's made that clear, but that's not a choice she's getting. I am his brother, as well as her uncle, and in this, I outrank her. If her mother – our sister, JJ's and mine, our big sister: *Angela, for fuck's sake* – if Angela were still alive, she'd outrank us all, and the entire funeral would be in her hands, which is a prospect I don't imagine Diana would find any more comforting. If Angela were alive, she'd be, she'd be ninety-six, but more to the point, if Angela were alive the chances of her being sober would be slimmer than a flamingo's shin. Which I suppose is why she's not alive in any case.

Diana snatches the paper from my hand, scans it quickly and hands it back. I can't read that, she says. There's nothing wrong with my handwriting, not now. It didn't help that you stole my pen, though, did it, JJ? Still, that Welsh night school bastard tortured it out of me. *You might have A-levels, Charlie Jellicoe, though God knows how, maybe you bribed the examiners? No? You wouldn't have had the money, would you? You may have A-levels, but you can't be a QS if no one can read your numbers, now can you, Charlie Jellicoe?* So my numbers are perfect, and the letters, the words, got dragged along behind, and still Diana says she can't read what I have written – so I read it myself, aloud, editing as I go: *The day my brother retired he killed a woman, not for the first time,* I don't mean a woman – well, okay, yes: a woman

she was a woman

And Diana says: You can't say that. ~I know, I say, these

3

days, it creates a certain . . . what's the word? . . . a certain *frisson*. She's looking blank. Come on, it's not that hard. ~Not frisson, I say, expectation, prejudice. It makes him sound like a monster. Diana slaps at the sheet of paper in my hand and the sound is surprisingly loud. ~It's a funeral, she says. You can't say he killed anyone.

He did, though. And – to be honest – it wasn't just a woman, was it? Not just any woman. Even if that really wasn't the point. Not the second time, anyway. That's what I was trying to get at – it's that he *never did anything else*. Which isn't right, either. I don't mean he only ever killed people. That would be stupid, nobody ever *only* kills people, do they, however bad or mad they are? We all have a hinterland. Even Hitler liked to paint, Uncle Joe wrote poetry and loved his mother. Truly. Pol Pot? I don't know. I can't be expected to keep tabs on every homicidal dictator, now can I? Not these days – *100 minus seven equals 93, minus seven equals 86* – no, what I mean is that, afterwards, after the second time, he never did anything again, and yes, I know, he did some things, he ate and slept and no doubt wiped his arse, or had it wiped for him, towards the end. He'd meet me sometimes, for a drink: not here, in town – when he could fit it in between that charity stuff he did, towards the end, the food banks, and the woman he met there – when we both still went up to town to drink instead of doing it all at home, in bed, from teacups. But that's not anything, really, is it? In thirty years? That's not a life.

If the first time was tragedy, the second was surely farce? And after that, after '86, he *withdrew*. For decades. What's charity, after all? The last refuge of the scoundrel. Ask Profumo.

So what am I supposed to say? Tomorrow. What am I supposed to say tomorrow? At Honor Oak crematorium. That's what you wanted, wasn't it? The fire. I don't get it myself. Maybe because there'll be enough of that where I'm heading, if you believe. I don't believe, of course I don't believe. What do you take me for, Diana? All the same. What I want, when it's my time – *it is my time* – I want a modest headstone – no, bugger that, an *immodest* headstone – in the corner of some ancient graveyard that Diana and the rest of them can feel guilty about neglecting for a year or two. Where little Dougie – Frances' Douglas, that is, a boy after my own heart – can take his own sprogs and say: that's your great uncle there – great-great uncle? – next to the grave of William Blake, or some such *éminence grise*. One of the more prominent Jellicoes, perhaps. A descendant of the first Earl Jellicoe himself. There's enough of the buggers around, and not one of them related to us, as far as we can tell. And little Dougie's offspring can look up at their father, tears in the corners of their bright blue eyes – eyes framed by perfect blond ringlets, I dare say – and lisp: What was great about him, Daddy? – *It's a great life if you don't weaken* – Does Dougie have children already? Does he? I think he might. I say already. He must be – what? – forty by now? Forty. Where are we? 2017 – so forty would make it 1977. That's about right. Sunny Jim Callaghan, Provo bombs in West End pubs; battering the NF in Lewisham and Brick Lane. See? There's nothing wrong with my memory, whatever the doctors think. Nothing. Even so. Even if I were to die to-morrow – which I won't, but even if I did – Dougie's nippers might be too old – if Dougie himself's already forty – too old for the charming vignette of Hallmark waifery I've just conjured out of nothing. They might be grunting teenagers who never hear a thing their father says because their ears are plugged straight into Cupertino, CA.

We're none of us getting any younger.

It's better than the alternative, I suppose.

You'd think I'd know. About Dougie. He's Frances' boy. You would think I'd know.

I can't die tomorrow, though can I, JJ? Because tomorrow's a date. Tomorrow we've got to vote. No. I mean, yes: vote – but then we've got to incinerate your corpse and scatter the grit on Peckham Rye. You were quite specific, at the end. And I've got to say a few words, and probably read something. Which, if Diana has her way, would probably be that Auden bollocks, but it won't. We're not stopping any clocks. Where would that leave us? – *It's a great life* – Dougie doesn't have children, does he? I remember now. He's queer as a nine bob note. Runs a club in Vauxhall. A boy after my own heart, or some such organ.

There's always Rochester. For the poem, I mean. Rochester, second Earl of: *Dead, we become the lumber of the world.* I could quote that. The lumber of the world. It was Bee who first told me about Rochester. And if she were there? Tomorrow. What would she say? That the man we are cremating is not the man she married, perhaps. But then, he never was. And if she read a poem? It'd be someone none of us had ever heard of. Some bright new hope from the inner-city borders of poetry and per-formance, perhaps. Is there still hope in poetry? In Rochester?

So what am I thinking, then? Me. Charlie Jellicoe. Peckham born and bred, orphan son of a Communist printer, mourn-ing my identical twin brother by quoting the second Earl of Rochester, purveyor of seventeenth-century aristo-smut? What made me this way? What? That's another story, not JJ's. Nothing makes us, nothing made me. If Bee were there, tomorrow, I'd greet her like I always did, a kiss upon each cheek, a hug if these old arms of mine are capable of such a thing. I'd have to put my stick down first. I liked Bee, even if her enthusiasm could be tiring – *this old* heart *of mine* – That's what it was. Not arms. The Isley Brothers, if I'm not mistaken, which I'm not, but you wouldn't think an old coffin-dodger like me would know this shit, would you? I do, though. I really do. A lifetime of Forces Favourites, Family Favourites, that never were my bloody favourites, but what did I care? Radio Caroline, Radio 1, Radio 2: once they invented transistors you never got much choice about what you heard on the building sites, all day. It just seeped in. And, for most people, just seeped out again, I guess. But me, I've somehow kept my finger, if not exactly on the pulse, then at least somewhere not too far from the rapidly-cooling corpse of popular culture. This old heart of mine. Weak? Broken?

Nah.

Diana says, That was thirty years ago. She means the last death. The last time JJ killed somebody. ~You're hoping everyone's forgotten? ~There's no need to mention it. ~But what else is there? She does that thing she does, tucking her hair behind her ears with both hands, running them around her jaw. It was cute when she was seventeen. She's been calling me Uncle Charlie for almost seventy years. Since I was seventeen myself, and more like a cousin, really, than an uncle – Sinatra. See? – *It was a very good year* . . . it bloody was, I tell you. Seventeen. It was 1948, the year the NHS was born, and all the rest of it. ~You're his brother, Uncle Charlie. *What am I supposed to say to that?* ~You should tell some stories about growing up together. Say how committed he was to building decent houses for the poor. Say you loved him. That's all anybody wants to hear. That's what she says, and . . . I nod. It's the longest speech I've heard her make in years. I give her

7

the impression that I think she's right, after all. That it really is that simple. I even say: You're right. Though we don't call ourselves *the poor* any more, do we? We don't. I'm not poor, not any more. And neither were you. But that's not what I mean. We talk about disadvantage and low-income families. At a pinch, we might just talk about poverty – as an abstract noun, like Beveridge's giant evils Want and Squalor – and, God help us, about social mobility, as if it was all about a few smart kids getting richer – *a few smart kids like us* – but never, not ever, about people being poor. About poor people. It's not polite. It's demeaning. As if being hungry enough to feed your kids from a food bank and living six to a mould-covered room you might get kicked out of tomorrow weren't demeaning enough, and – I don't say any of this – Diana smiles and clicks her teeth, relieved. ~I'll be here about ten to pick you up. *I get around.* I could get there on the Easy Rider. Not a bad way to turn up at a funeral. Pale horse, be damned. ~Don't worry, I say. ~It's no trouble, she says. Except it is, isn't it? For her. Driving through the Rotherhithe Tunnel at rush hour. I can't think what possessed her to move to Mile End. A man? A job? ~I'm going to vote first, I say. You should, too. I don't say *It's what he would have wanted* – which would be laying it on too thick, even for Diana. She says she supposes so, though it won't make much difference where she lives. It won't make much difference here, either. Harriet-bloody-Harman isn't going to lose a twenty-five thousand-vote majority. ~That's not the point, I say, piously. We vote: it's what we do. There's nothing she can say to that. She offers me tea; I decline. And so she leaves, at last. But on her way downstairs, she says: I'll see you at ten. And shuts the door behind her.

It's 4.15pm. I have eighteen hours. Surely that's enough?

What about a drink, to lubricate the gears? Not yet. It's

only teatime. Not that I've ever been one for all that sun below the yardarm bollocks. A drink's a drink, whether it's ten in the morning or ten at night. How long is it we've had all-day opening? Years. Decades? Possibly. Wasn't it Blair? Opening hours never meant that much to me. Don't get me wrong, I loved pubs. Still do. I love the noise on a Friday night, and the quiet on a Tuesday afternoon. I love the bevelled glass and the polished wood, the peanuts and crisps and the barmaids you can flirt with and the young men at the bar who don't flirt, at least not with barmaids, and the landlord banging the bell and telling us all to bugger off, and, yes, he does mean bugger. I love the beer and whisky, the brandy and the gin. It's just, for me, pubs have never been the only – or even the best – place to drink, and – *I'll tell you what else happened in 1948. Larry Olivier made Hamlet.* This I know I know because Angela dragged us to the Tower on Rye Lane to see it twice because, she said, it might help us with our exams, and after that she always thought she was quoting the Prince of Denmark on a Saturday night when she said: *There's nothing either good or bad, but drinking makes it so.* She was wrong, of course. She had what Diana might call a problem with alcohol, if Diana could ever bring herself to talk about her mother. (The problem being, naturally, that she couldn't get enough. Ba-bum-tish.) Then JJ and I grew up, and her kids grew up and she discovered that booze was more important than paying the bills, and it wasn't a problem for a while. For most of the 60s she was fun to be with, as long as you got to her early in the day. Which was fine by me. I had other things to do at night. Then the bank tried to repossess Tony's Hillman Hunter, and all of a sudden it was a problem. You tried to stop me seeing your mother, then, didn't you, Diana? You said I was an enabler. Even Frances told me I had to stop bringing sherry, and – I listened then, because it was Frances, Angela and Tony's second, more lovable daughter, but – *you were never the problem, were you JJ? Never an enabler?* – I place both hands on the head of my stick and lever myself out of my chair. It's a knobkerrie. The stick. A beautiful word – a beautiful thing. Ash, or birch, or some such. I'm not really one for trees. It's none too practical for hands as palsied and cramped as mine, but beautiful all the same. I tell Diana I keep it because, if push came to shove, and shove to assault, I could still crack a man's skull with its heavy, polished knob. She doesn't believe me. These days I mostly use it round the flat. I keep the Rollator by the door. A walking frame with wheels and a nifty fold-down canvas seat for when the walking gets too much. I try not to use the scooter unless I have to, even though it's an Easy Rider and cool as fuck, as I believe the saying is. Or was. *I get around.* I keep the stick because, beneath it all, I am a sentimental fool. I hobble to the kitchen, fill the kettle at the adapted tap and make the tea I refused from Diana.

Back at the table, I place the hot mug carefully on an almost antique coaster with the word PRIDE in fake old-timey print capitals like the lettering on a wanted poster. Except rainbow-coloured. What would Mum have thought of that?

She'd probably have been made up to see you use a coaster.

I look again at the page I've written. I squint. Perhaps Diana has a point. Am I going to be able to read this tomorrow? In my experience the lighting in crematoria is not too bright. Perhaps I should type? I have a laptop Dougie bought me. I can print things in huge fonts, thirty-six, forty-eight-point type, so that's what I will do. I take the computer out of its case and boot it up, and while it's doing whatever it is they do that takes so long, I fold the handwritten sheet I'd shown Diana and tear it in half, but carefully, carefully. I can always type it out again.

The trouble is, there was nothing else. Nothing after. But what about before? Is Diana right? Or maybe not just boyhood stuff, but all the way back. *Ab ovo*, a teacher who couldn't tell JJ and me apart, once told us. He wasn't alone. Tony couldn't, either. I'm not sure Angela was always sure, but – *anyway* – the teacher got sidetracked onto twins in history. He told the class about Leda and the Swan, and the eggs; about the twins Castor and Pollux and about Helen without whom, he said, stressing the 'm', sphinctering his lips as if kissing an aunt, without *whom*, no abduction, no Trojan War. Hence the phrase, he said. ~What phrase? we said. ~*Ab ovo*. Meaning? ~From the egg, sir. ~Good. From the egg, yes. But, figuratively, from the beginning. The origin. The cause. I could start again from the moment, perhaps, the twin moments, I should say, of our births. Me, the eldest; he, Jolyon, decidedly not clutching at my heel, a reluctant Jacob to my Esau: *my brother is an hairy man*, or was: I am the smooth one. Or so it is alleged. Whose birthright was whose? I am older. This should not be happening. Ten minutes I had her to myself, before you came along. Except I didn't really, did I? She was up to her eyes in you, flat on her back on the kitchen table – she wasn't going to ruin the bloody mattress, was she? – ten minutes pushing and screaming like a banshee, the midwife looking to me, tying off the cord and calling to her: Push! You're nearly there, you're nearly there, push! Push! And Mother screaming back blue murder: fuck, fuck, I'm pushing! Fuck fuck fuuuuuuuuuuuuuuuuuuuuuuuuucccccckkkkk! Is that any way to meet your mother? To be introduced? And what was it all for? All that fuss? Because, let's face it, JJ, you were the easy one, the one who slipped into the world, and slipped through life. I was the one causing all the pain.

And where might Dad have been, while all this was going on? Well, it was late at night her labour started, and about four in the afternoon before the whole grisly business was done. Time for tea and cake, though there wasn't often cake. Four on a sweltering afternoon in the high summer of 1931, it was, so I imagine he wouldn't be home for another couple of hours, at least, if it was a weekday. I don't know. Do you? I only know the time because Mum told us, whenever she wanted to rub it in. So he'd have been home about six, or much later if there was a branch meeting that night, or a committee for the defence of this or that, or red and black leaflets and posters to print, after hours, once Manny, the owner, Mr. Levinson that is, had left. He was Dad's boss, but also his friend – which was ironic, really, Dad having a boss for a friend: but Manny, Mr. Levinson, was never what you'd call a capitalist – *more of a kulak, perhaps* – and once he went home he turned a blind eye and left Dad to it, the presses still running, the keys in a bunch hanging underneath the counter. In which case, it might have been hours, midnight, before Dad got home and found that, ten years after Angela, he'd finally become a dad again. Ten years.

So burying Angela made sense to me. She raised us; we'd bury her. The way it's supposed to go. At least till Tony got up and read the kind of eulogy I'll be buggered if I'll read tomorrow. Lot of vapid nonsense. I don't even know what he was doing there. She'd left him. So what, they never divorced? She'd left: at least, she hadn't gone home. Not for the last couple of years. Pillar of the community, my arse. He might as well have been the vicar. We swore then, JJ and me, we swore we wouldn't let that happen to us, to each other. We swore, like we were ten years old again, newly orphaned, cutting our palms and mingling our blood, but – *I never believed I'd bury him.* I'm older. Surely it should fall to you to bury me, JJ? Perhaps you thought the same. No one wants to be last, and, really, there's nothing to choose between us, actuarially speaking. It could have been me. *I could have been you.* Tell me you know what I mean? I drank more, but gave up smoking earlier. These things surely cancel each other out? We should have gone together. That would have been better. A plane crash, maybe, though it's been years since anyone would let either of us on a plane. A freak meteor strike at a family picnic? I'm not sure which is less likely, the meteor or the picnic.

When Tony finished, we read poems we'd brushed up for the occasion. Me: Herbert. You: Larkin. Which was sly of you, I thought. Of course, you had no more children than me, or the librarian of Hull. Angela had two: Diana and Frances. Our mother, three: Angela, when she was young; and then, when she really wasn't, you and me together, and neither of us tiny. We must have nearly been the death of her.

So she said, often enough.
But surely never meant.

It was cheese, in the end, that was the death of her, and of our father, not us. Or stout. Or something that roiled her dyspepsia and brought her bolt upright at four am – something else she left me – when she'd only gone to bed at half past two. It kept her awake until she thought she might as well get up and make a cup of tea, or Horlicks, or whatever it was that made her light the gas at a quarter to five, or thereabouts, and – *wasn't that Ronan Point?* – the all-clear had sounded just before two: they'd survived, again. She wasn't to know a direct hit a couple of houses up the road had left a bomb that wouldn't explode until it was found and carted away years later, but which had nonetheless ruptured a pipe and filled her kitchen with gas – *1968? Some other mother?* – I forget. Let's nudge the Heinkel's bombsight up a fraction of a degree and – there we go: our house obliterated with appropriate dignity.

JJ sighed, the last time we discussed this, our funerals. Who'd go first. For some people, I remember saying, the world is made afresh each morning. ~Isn't it, you said. ~Maybe, but it bores us to tears all the same.

The last time? I don't forget. The doctors' questions are always the same. ~*Can you tell me who the Prime Minister is, Mr. Jellicoe?* ~*May, Cameron, Brown, Blair.* ~*Excellent. Now can you count down from a hundred in sevens?* ~*Of course I can. There's nothing wrong with me. More's the pity.*

It was – what? Ten years ago? Less. You'd started in at the food bank by then, dishing out Pot Noodles to victims of Universal Credit. You talked about Momentum. Momentum, for Christ's sake! It was like your second childhood. We met in a pub on Old Compton Street that had been blown apart a decade earlier – *I'll get back to that* – in the late afternoon, the light outside already more neon than sunshine. Four men, all middle-aged – younger than us, at any rate – sat at two separate tables, each of them scrolling wordlessly through mobile phones. ~For Christ's sake, people! I said, too loudly. Drink. Eat! Laugh! They ignored me, in that careful way we all ignore people – even harmless old men like me – who shout in pubs in the afternoon. JJ, too. JJ sipped his whisky and ignored me. ~You're going to die. You know that, right? *Of course they knew.* ~You're going to fucking die. *Which didn't mean they'd want to talk about it.* ~Make the best of it, I said, defeated. You asked if I remembered you once asking me if I enjoyed life. ~Of course I remember, I said. Were we drunk? ~We'd had a drink, you said. Of course we had. It had been 1960-something. Even then we were too old for that sort of conversation. ~I remember, I said. You asked if I enjoyed my life. Not Life. No capital L. My life. And I said: Of course. What else was there? And you said: Purpose. Meaning. And I said –

~You said: Where's the fun in that?

Now – by which I mean: then, on Old Compton Street, some years ago – it was 2012 or so and we, JJ and I, who'd never really believed we'd see the twenty-first century, and never really believed it when we did, we watched those four men put away their mobile phones and leave, two-by-two. And we kept watching, kept drinking our whisky, while six more men – younger, more attractive men – arrived. Such is life. What can you do? What can anybody do?

How much of this can I repeat tomorrow?

There's love, of course. Purpose, meaning, he said, but never mentioned love, even though that was one thing he did have in his life, whatever happened later.

My tea is cold. It is five p.m. Time for *P.M.* May, Cameron, Brown. And after tomorrow? Corbyn? Fat chance. Improbable, to say the least. Eddie Mair can wait.

There's love. And marriage. Of course. Putting the horse before the carriage. An autumn wedding, for reasons I can't recall. Not everything's still there. If my brother chose to get hitched in October, who am I to second-guess his motives? Or Bee's? Or – more likely, now I think of it – Bee's mother, "Lady" Antonia's, motives. Shotguns were not involved, I know that much. Her family approved of JJ, in their own way. He was a working class boy - no longer a boy - but this was 1959, and there'd be room at the top for a grammar school lad with a degree, with National Service behind him and a bright, bright future ahead, rebuilding Britain. I dare say they'd have preferred a proper profession - an architect selling to the council, perhaps, rather than working for it. What exactly did a housing manager *do*? Was that a new thing? And wasn't it a shame not to *use* his degree? To be a smooth, and not an hairy man. But even Tories loved slum clearance in 1959. And if JJ insisted on working in the inner city, they could put that, too, down to the spirit of the times. You were amiable enough, then, weren't you? Idealistic, yes, but you were young, "Lady" Antonia said, and you never shoved it down their throats. Meaning: not like your brother, not even like their daughter. You'd be a steadying influence on Beatrice. Total bollocks, but she wished it so.

And what of me, then? I'd have been cool, of course, in the oyster-grey Continental-cut single-breasted suit that Tomas-the-tailor had persuaded me into, with its short jacket and lapels so narrow and so sharp I could slice my fingers open just fastening the mother-of-pearl clip on my green silk tie. The hat? No hat. This was 1959. The year of the M1 and Ronnie Scott's. We were the future. My collection of hom-burgs, trilbies and fedoras - lovingly gathered and preserved since I'd left the RAF and begun buying my own clothes (or having them bought by grateful friends) - had been temp-orarily demoted to the back of the wardrobe, along with the box-back double-breasted suits with shoulder pads like rocket fins and chalk stripes like aircraft landing strips. Fashion is fickle, I knew: their time would come again. But I wouldn't have been in one of my suits, would I? Because it was your wedding, yours and Bee's, and for all you thought yourself the future, the modern man, you'd decided, or agreed with Bee's mother – against Bee's better judgment, I would guess; which says a lot, in retrospect. Her parents were paying for everything, after all, everything except the ring, which had been our mother's – *no it hadn't: Mum had been blown to smithereens and we weren't around to sift the remains for usable accessories* – and you'd agreed, decided, agreed to go for morning dress from Moss Bros. Now, it wouldn't be the first time I'd worn a suit that had been worn before by another man, but it *was* the first time I hadn't met the man in question first, hadn't stood at his wardrobe, flicking idly through the hangers waiting for him to say: the *blue*, I think, on you, or perhaps the – no, not that one, darling, it was a present. Or hadn't rifled brazenly through another's collection while he, no doubt thinking our relationship more than it was, foolishly left me alone in his flat while he took care of business somewhere in the City, or Whitehall, or wherever. My point being that I was not wholly agin the whiff of another man. I *liked* the faint odour of alien bodily fluids that could be released when least expected, when the fabric was brushed or creased by sudden movement. It could be romantic. There I'd be, stuck in some municipal office with a huddle of recalcitrant town planners, transported with a Proustian rush to a different world of illicit pleasure. But I'm getting ahead of myself. The point being that, no, I wasn't bothered about going to my brother's wedding in a suit that wasn't mine, but there was a world of difference between appropriating another man's tailoring – from each according to his ability; to each according to his needs, after all – and the cab-rank, pseudo-democracy of wearing clothes that have been worn by any old body with sufficient dosh to hire them. It's the difference between a Soho members' club and a Gents toilet. I've never been a snob, but I've always picked and chosen, and I've never been a whore.

I told JJ and Beatrice I was not happy. Bee said, Moss Bros was good enough for the Coronation. ~Good enough for Ramsay Macdonald, too, said JJ. They kitted him up for visits to the Palace. ~I bet they didn't stuff him in trousers steeped in the sweat of a dozen commercial reps, though, did they? ~They do clean them, Charlie. Which wasn't much better. Well, it was, I suppose, but still. I said: They'll *dry clean* them. ~Exactly, JJ said. ~So they'll stink like ICI and be brittle to the touch. When I was introduced to Tomas - the best gift anyone ever gave me, by the way, from a man I can't remember anything else about - and Tomas made the first suit ever made especially for me, he insisted dry cleaning was an abomination. Nothing would ruin the wool or the hang of well-made clothes more effectively than the solvents and steam presses those charlatans employ. Tetrachloroethylene was not his idea of style, and consequently not mine, either. In all but the most extreme cases, he declared - the spillage by a tipsy waiter of a whole tureen of borscht into one's lap, for instance - it is better to sponge clean with a damp cloth and hand press with a domestic iron. Better still, naturally, to have one's valet do it, but I was never in that class, and never wanted to be. Tomas knew that. He was only teasing. He was Hungarian and one of the few straight tailors I've ever met with any real claim to flair. His shop was in Bermondsey. Not because he couldn't have been in Savile Row, but because that's where he chose to be, and considered he had chosen well. He felt no need to move. Come the wedding, JJ said: You could have yours made, if you can afford it: Bee's dad isn't going to pay for that. He knew I couldn't afford it. It would be some years before I could settle Tomas' bills myself. ~You'd have to make JJ's too,

Bee said. They have to match. ~Do they? Why? It had been a month or two of heavy outlay, what with the wedding present and the deposit on the double room in Bute Street. I wasn't keen to spend money on a suit I'd never wear again. It wasn't as if I'd be getting married myself. Still, I tried to imagine the look on Tomas' face if I took him JJ's rental and asked him to copy it for me. ~They just do, Bee said. The fitting's next Thursday. ~I thought it was this week? JJ said. ~No, sweetheart. The eighth. Mum sent you the appointment card.

We were in JJ's room at the time, the one in Deptford, before he moved – before the council knocked the whole street down. I was sitting on the bed because there were only two chairs. There were boxes stacked under the bed, under the sink, under the small table. One balanced precariously on top of the hot water geyser. Boxes of leaflets and posters straight from the printers.

~But that's election day. ~I know. ~How could you? ~I didn't. Mum did. ~Of course she did. She wouldn't want us getting out the Labour vote, now, would she? ~You're being silly, JJ. We knew you'd both be taking the day off anyway, and it won't take long. We're going over to Mum's afterwards, so we could canvas there. It'll do more good than here.

The wedding would be in South Ken, where Bee's parents lived. Not far from Bute Street, as it happened, at least as the crow flies. And not far from North Kensington, either, where George Rogers had been the Labour MP since the war. But there had been riots in Notting Hill that summer, the Union Movement was all over the place, and Mosley himself was standing. ~Oh, goody, I said. We can wear the morning suits to fight fascists. That'll confuse the *Daily Mail*. JJ said there wouldn't be any fighting. ~Pretty please? ~Discipline comrade, said Bee, and winked. JJ said, And I can't canvas anywhere. Which was true. He worked for a council. Sticking up posters was one thing, knocking on doors asking people to vote Labour was another. It wasn't against the law, then, but he was always very conscious of how things looked, of his own professionalism. I could get away with it, because no one knew who I was. But JJ was already getting too high up. And no one could tell us apart. Bee said, So what's the problem?

I know it's hard to believe, Dougie, for someone like you, born when you were – someone not old – hard to believe that 1950s elections were fought over who would build the most houses. 200,000 *a year? I see your* 200,000 *says Macmillan, and raise you* 300,000. *Ah, but what* kind *of houses,* Bevan says. Bevan, who lost the election in '51 by building houses too good to go up fast enough. Nothing was too good for the working classes, Bevan said, and he was right. But now they'd get smaller houses, built by private developers, not by councils, built by Wilmots and the rest of them – but at least they'd be houses, and hundreds of thousands of working people would have somewhere to live. Somewhere warm and dry, where the running water was in the taps not down the walls. That's all we ever wanted, wasn't it? – *not really* – But Bee was right, Dougie, I *had* booked the day off. I'd booked the Friday, too. Just in case. There might be alcohol involved on election night, whichever way the vote went, and a degree of celebration of the brotherhood of man, and – *you* know what I mean, Dougie, don't you?

So, then. October 1959. We're being shepherded up King Street, JJ and me, with Bee, as usual, playing shepherdess, up past the Communist Party offices at number 16, to Moss Bros, which, as fate and the London property market would have it, was in those days just across the road. From the outfitters' windows we could look down on the comrades coming and going as we waited to be measured. ~Dad might have been one of them, JJ said. ~So why aren't you? I said, and: ~Why aren't you? he replied. ~Because you've both got too much sense, said Beatrice the schoolteacher. You both want to really get things done. ~How do you know? I said. ~Because you say so. Every single day. ~I mean, how do you know I'm not a Party member? ~*You*? JJ spluttered. ~Me. ~What? Shilling for Uncle Joe? ~Stalin's dead, brother Jolyon. His mistakes have been acknowledged. Do keep up. ~And Hungary's full of Soviet tanks. ~Details, details, I said. (Which was not what I'd said to Tomas.) ~Surely, Bee said, your dad would have left by now?

We couldn't be sure, though, could we? We couldn't *know*. Dad's loyalty had survived the Nazi-Soviet pact, after all. He'd made the switch from Popular Front to opposing the imperialist war, but so did plenty of others who would later baulk at Hungary, or Prague. He didn't even get the satisfaction of seeing the Party make it all right to fight fascists again, because by then the fascists had already killed him. So who knows?

I said: You'd be surprised who you meet. And there's nothing sexier than a double life. Even Bee looked as if she wished I wouldn't say such things in public. I said, It was them or the Freemasons. Which might have been more use at work, but would really have had Dad spinning in his grave, if there'd been anything left to spin. It should have been JJ, really, with the double life. A youthful fling with the Young Communists at university, before a tap on the shoulder, a job at the Foreign Office and, three decades later, a midnight flit to Moscow. Maybe the architecture school at UCL wasn't that kind of place? We might have been hurtling towards a meritocracy, but treachery still took class.

An overweight young man with carefully buffed fingernails

brought out two suits for us to try. We've always been wide for our height, you and I, or short for our girth. Like trolls. The trousers puddled around our feet and the sleeves flapped over our second knuckles. Bee could barely stifle a giggle. The assistant assured us he could find a better fit; if necessary the trousers could be taken up. ~Which of you, he asked again, is the groom? ~Me, said I, winking at Bee. There might as well be some fun to be had out of this, after all. Even JJ played along. It would make no difference. ~Darling, I said, and took Bee's hand when the assistant suggested a patterned waistcoat, What *would* your mother say?

We never made much use of being identical, did we JJ? Not when we were young. Once or twice, at school, and on the farm during the war, I'd managed to get out of trouble by sowing doubt. *It must have been my brother. Not me.* More often, we'd get a beating just the same. For being the same, for *not* being different, for causing confusion and unease among our peers. There's a reason horror films are full of twins. Our early lives were not a riot of hilarious mistaken-identity japes. When I say my brother was an hairy man, I don't mean it literally, any more than Jacob did, I suppose.

And I did go canvassing that afternoon. JJ wasn't happy, but he didn't have to do it, did he? He was not his brother's keeper. I met plenty of hairy men in Notting Hill, and a couple of hairy women, too. On the doorstep, there was a sullen, defensive mood about. Meaning some of those who said they wouldn't vote for Mosley, would. And those who said they would, did so without any prompting, belligerently, as if frustrated at repeating an argument they'd been having with themselves. ~My husband didn't fight in the war, one woman said, the moment she opened the door on a quiet street of dilapidated three-storey terraces, before I could say a word, He didn't die fighting Nazis – she said it 'NAR-zees', like Churchill used to – to have me live next door to a bunch of stinking nig-nogs. I backed away. Canvassing isn't about changing people's minds. ~This used to be a decent street. Now? Now I wouldn't piss on it if it was burning down.

Now? Now she'll be dead. And her house – it wouldn't have been her house, mind; she probably just rented a couple of rooms – if it wasn't torn down in the 60s, that house would be worth a couple of million. At least. So I hope the man next door – a suave black man about my own age in a dou-ble-breasted suit, tan co-respondent shoes and a tie that lit up West London by itself, who opened the door before I could even knock and said politely that he'd already voted Labour, as had his father and his brothers, all the while ignoring the vitriol his neighbour spat in his ear – I hope that man lives there still, with his children and his grandchildren, if that's what they want. I hope he has stayed sharp. I hope he bought it early and that house has made him rich. Even if I don't believe houses should make anybody rich. I hope his mother and his sisters voted, too.

Diana and the doctors seem to think it's a bad sign, that remembering who wore what, who said what, who did what in 1959 – or '39 or '68 or '86 – must be a symptom of something going wrong, of my decline, of me becoming detached from the present, from who said what this morning. They're wrong. They don't know me. Well, Diana knows me, but maybe she's forgotten – she's no spring chicken herself – I've always been like this. I remember what Baldie the gatekeeper at the Pioneer Centre was really called. (Mr. Hayes to you, sonny). I remem-ber what Angela said after the war when she wanted to move out of Peckham and I said I'd had enough of the country. (She said: Not country, country: Bromley.) I remember what I said when Dad came home and told us about a rent strike in a block just off Rye Lane, where he'd helped the tenants barricade themselves into the flats, and stayed eight weeks; that's how long it took. When the landlord turned up, they arrested him and staged a trial, right there in the courtyard. (I said: Was he guilty?) We were only four, JJ and me, but I remember that, I swear I do. The landlord was called Himmelschein, and when Mosley's mob turned up, trying to make something out of that, they got driven off with bags of flour and bottles and bricks, and Dad said he personally flattened William Joyce with an empty beer bottle outside the Heaton Arms. But he told us that later, in September 1939, when Joyce – Lord Haw-Haw – was all over the radio.

I remember. The Heaton Arms is a block of flats these days.

I remember VE Day – who doesn't? – but I remember what JJ said when he heard the news.

Now we'll have to go home.
That's right. I remember all the words to 'Moon River': Audrey Hepburn, *Breakfast at Tiffany's*. I remember what she said, the day JJ retired. I remember what Tiresias saw: like him, I've walked among the lowest of the dead.

It's not a gift.

But it's not surprising, is it? Not a sign of any cognitive deterioration on my part, that I remember what Bee said, when I told you both I was leaving the council to work for Wilmots. She said I couldn't worship God and Mammon. She really did. I laughed. Even though I couldn't breathe and thought I might be about to die, because we were in the middle of a demo, a riot, crushed against the temporary barricades outside St Pancras Town Hall. I said: I don't worship anyone, Bee. Except you. She smiled, the sort of smile you

24

pour over a puppy, while police on horses with big fucking sticks were Light Brigading-it up Euston Road, battering shit out of protesters, a hail of missiles raining down on them, and us. What were we doing there? Building the New Jerusalem, if I remember. ~*Wasn't that the day job, Uncle Charlie?* ~*Well, that's the point, Dougie. A point, anyway. It's what your Uncle JJ said.* ~*Great uncle.* He said we shouldn't be there, couldn't be there. We were council employees. But it wasn't our council, and Bee wasn't having it. They'd been married a year; this wasn't the first demo she'd press-ganged him into. We'd been here the year before, on this very corner, when Labour ran St Pancras and were flying the red flag from the Town Hall and supporting the *worker's bomb*. When they were breaking the law, refusing to put up rents. When fascists broke up a Council meeting, chucking leaflets in Bee's face. The leaflets said we had to get rid of the yids. Being a council employee didn't stop your Uncle JJ breaking that fascist's nose, Dougie, but it did make him slink off pretty sharpish afterwards. ~*And you?* ~*Me?* I was the communist, but it was Bee who got us out onto the streets. What were we doing there? Fighting for housing – housing was the heart of everything, Dougie. It always is. And it's true what I told you, about Labour and the Tories outbidding each other, but it was never the whole story. It never is. Their lot built houses, but cut subsidies. Abolished controls and watched rents rocket. There were council tenants stuck in requisitioned houses since the war, and the landlords jacked up their rents. St Pancras agreed to pay the difference, while the government cut the rates they could raise – *I know, Dougie, I know: local government finance. That'll really liven up a funeral* – but in 1958, Dougie, in 1959 and '60 there was fighting in the streets about this stuff. ~Really? ~Don't say really; but, yes. When the Tories took St Pancras, they tripled the rents, and the General Election that year, the one I'd been canvassing in – and JJ hadn't – was a Tory landslide. Labour held North Ken, and Mosley came fourth of four, but a couple of thousand people voted for him, all the same

despite your efforts.

Tripled the rents, Dougie.

I know, I know . . . but that's why we were in the Euston Road getting crushed and battered. We were lobbying the Housing Committee. There was a rent strike going on your granddad would have been proud of. But the ringleaders – Don Cook, Arthur Rowe: and one of them a communist, Dougie, believe me – they were getting ready for the end. Their flats were ringed around with barbed wire, guarded by twenty-four hour pickets and barricaded with lumber, old furniture and pianos – pianos, Dougie! God knows where they got them – a dozen inside one small flat. Anything to make it harder for the cops. They put the kettle on and waited. Outside, around the Town Hall, fists and bricks and spears of ripped up railings flew like Agincourt, while your Great-uncle JJ – *who didn't want to be there* – and Great-Aunt Bee – shoulders back, face beaming with conviction: she would've made a perfect Suffragette or, even earlier, a knitter of woollen helmets for our young men in the Crimea – JJ and Bee and I discussed my career options between baton charges and renditions of the Red Flag.

~Wilmots build houses, I said. That's what we want, isn't it? ~Houses for rich people, Bee said, and we ducked, together, as a policeman's helmet came flying into the crowd. ~Rich people *and* poor people, I said. They build for councils. That's why they want me. ~To help them fleece councils. ~Oh, come on, Bee. The council pays JJ. The council pays Wilmots, and Wilmots pays me. What's the difference?

26

Did I really say this, in the middle of a riot?

I thought I knew the difference, then.

JJ said, How much? ~No more than I'm getting now. JJ tried to mime incredulity, but had to bend double as a concrete flower tub, ripped down from a wall and heaved towards a mounted copper overshot its mark, and crashed into the wall behind us. When Bee had hauled us back up and shaken the soil out of her hair she said: Then why are you doing it? Why, indeed? It was a reasonable question, Dougie. I'd told them the truth about the salary. But it wasn't the money. It really wasn't.

What, then?

Don't think I didn't ask myself a thousand times. The best I could do was: I was bored. - *I know. But I was* - I'd been impatient, Dougie. Hard to imagine, isn't it, now that it takes me twenty minutes to hobble to the kitchen and put the kettle on, but there you go. I'd wanted to get on. Not up. I wasn't looking for the room at the top. I wanted to get stuff done. So when we finished school and your Uncle JJ went on to study architecture, I thought I'd crack on, get national service out the way, get bloody moving. After two years in the RAF I went straight into the council. And night school. Which was hell, but I did it. Then JJ finally started work and didn't just catch up, Dougie, he went shooting past. I watched him fit in and get on, knocking all the edges off his personality, so I said, then, on the Euston Road, I said: It might be fun. ~Fun? *Fun.* To her mother's horror, Bee was a primary school teacher. She should have understood the importance of fun.

The following morning, before dawn, police and bailiffs raided the two flats, smashing their way through the walls of one and the ceiling of the other. In Kentish Town, Don Cook waited with a friend while, outside, comrades pelted the police with bricks and poured oil from the roof like some mediaeval siege. Ninety minutes later the Old Bill finally made it past the last piano. They found Cook and his mate in the cramped kitchen, brewing up. He offered them a cup of tea. He might have been a communist, but by God he was an English communist, and – the Home Secretary banned demonstrations altogether, banned any assembly of two or more persons across the entire borough. For three months. In theory, you could have been nicked for buying an evening paper outside King's Cross. ~How can he? Bee wanted to know. Does he have the power?

Turned out he did. Emergency powers, designed to keep Mosley's fascists off the streets in 1936, as it happens. ~It wasn't the Home Office that beat the blackshirts, was it, Dougie? ~It wasn't, Uncle Charlie. ~No, it wasn't. Who was it, Dougie? ~Great-granddad. ~And thousands like him, Dougie. It wasn't all your great-granddad.

It wasn't all JJ, either. Not the building, or the falling down.

Fun? What on earth had I meant by that?

Is it still not six o'clock? I suppose that's a relief. I've a long way to go yet.

I suppose, if I'm honest, that I meant sex.

Honest?

Give me some leeway, JJ. I know this isn't about honesty. Tomorrow isn't. It's about you. About the great JJ, our memories of JJ.

Keep telling yourself that.

Oh, I shall.

There is a faint scratching at the door downstairs, as if some large rodent were inching a nose out of its burrow after a long winter's hibernation. A capybara, perhaps. Are capybaras rodents? Do they hibernate? Probably not. A key in the lock. It is not a rodent, it is Diana coming back – summoned like a supernatural being by my thoughts of tomorrow, not so much an avenging angel as the spirit of a schoolteacher reminding me the homework's due in the morning. What has she forgotten now? ~Uncle Charlie, she calls up the stairs, it's only me. *Who else would it be?* She had red hair when she was young and was pretty in a country cousin sort of way, even if she'd never seen the countryside. ~I forgot my glasses. Of course she did. And I'm the one whose memory they think they have to test. *May, Cameron, Brown. The second Earl Jellicoe resigned from the Cabinet in 1973, for the usual reasons.* She's coming up the staircase now, hanging on to the bannisters, pausing just enough to let me hear it every three or four steps. This flat is on two floors. A maisonette, you might say, if you could bring yourself to use such a word. A duplex (ditto). Whatever it is, it is not flat, as Diana never fails to remind me. The iron staircase spirals up from the hallway straight into my living room, and Diana emerges, like Venus from the - *what am I saying?* - like an elderly misfit from some 70s TV sci-fi show. She pauses, catches her breath, and doesn't have to say it, because she has said it so often before: Why do I insist on living here? Why do I - who cannot walk a yard without my stick, or ten yards without my Rollator, I who keep a mobility scooter outside my ground floor bedroom door - why do I insist on living in a flat with a spiral staircase?

Diana herself, my little niece, Diana lives in a ground floor flat that has a ramp instead of steps. She says it's best to be prepared. Given one of her hips isn't actually hers, but came straight from a titanium ball bearing factory in the former DDR, I guess she has a point.

But me? I live here because I still can, just, and because this spot here - where I'm sitting now, on a Wednesday evening in June 2017, with the summer sun spilling glorious London light over the telephone exchange across the way, pouring it through the trees to fill my room with gold - this spot here was part of the Long Room that stretched from one end of the Centre to the other, its cork floor perfect for Saturday night dances, or for five year-old boys to run and fall and not hurt ourselves, or to stand and watch, or to look down on the swimming pool where dads played water polo as if their lives depended on it, and wonder, again, how such a miracle of light and steel and glass could exist here, in filthy Peckham, exist just yards from Dennett's Road - from home

– and how it could be, for a few years, more home than home itself, until it closed, in 1939, requisitioned to make aircraft parts. We had to leave – *with wandering steps and slow* – and, when we returned, after the war, JJ and I, we couldn't go back, but the Centre itself reopened, the experiment continued, for a while, until the NHS caught up with it and stamped it out. We could have – but Angela wasn't interested. She was older, fourteen when Mum signed us up, and she'd never liked the place. And now – then – when *we* were fourteen, all she wanted for us was school. We were going to stay on, we were doing A-levels and we were bloody well passing, get it, JJ and me, we were going to bloody pass, the first of the Jellicoes ever. Our Jellicoes. I don't suppose the second Earl left Winchester with nothing but a GCE in woodworking. Angela was going to make something of us. And by then what Angela wanted was what mattered. It's still here, though, the Centre, with its floor-to-ceiling windows, its gymnasium and its pool, its brilliant white curved glass and steel exterior, its entry phone on the gate that wasn't there in 1939 – it was just Baldie then, who only pretended to be fierce – even if now it's flats, and the Long Room has been carved up, and Dennett's Road isn't there at all. Well, it is. The street is, the Earl of Derby is, and the one that used to be the Rising Sun – *how often pubs survived both the Blitz and Brutalism!* – but the houses aren't, not at our end, anyway. Ours wasn't the only direct hit. When I heard the council had redeveloped the Centre I knew I had to get hold of the best flat I could. Whatever Angela might have thought; whatever you said – and who were you to disapprove? Living still, after a fashion, then, alive if not exactly kicking, in Phoenix Gardens among all the ghosts of the Rochester Estate? Who were you to cast judgment?

No fucker. That's who.

So.

I think I meant sex. By fun I meant sex.

I know it now, even if I told myself something different then. The prospect of sex, the thrill of flirtation and the chase, the knowing look, the slowing step, the sweating palm and the tongue-tied dry-as-sandpaper mouth that just wasn't there for me in the council offices of south London with their Marges and their Bettys and their NALGO men's nights and their obsession with football and beer. Not that I had anything against men or football or beer – two out of three ain't bad, anyway – but it was just *dreary, dearie.* There was sex everywhere and nowhere, in all the conversations that weren't actually about work, and even a few that were. But would any of them have let me put their cock in my mouth? And even if they would – and I could probably have tried harder – would I have wanted to?

I didn't say that, then, in the middle of a riot, to my brother, who worked in the same offices, or to his infinitely more attractive wife. I said I thought by going to work for Wilmots I'd meet more interesting people. As if that were any better, any less insulting. What I meant, of course, was better-looking people – present company excepted, as I didn't say – better-dressed people, people with different ideas about what life was for and different attitudes to risk and throwing it all away because it might just be a laugh. The CP wasn't any better, to be honest, whatever I'd said. Better people, mostly. Inspiring people, some of them, committed champions of the cause and courageous, implacable opponents of the boss class and their fascist attack dogs, naturally – along with a fair scattering of tedious, monotonous fantasists, like any organization, I imagine, that is fundamentally opposed to what exists. People I sincerely loved and respected – and a few I hated, again naturally – but none of them interesting in the way I meant interesting, not in my branch, anyway. I never met Kim Philby. There may have been a Fifth Man, but I never knew numbers one to four. When I said interesting I meant people – let's not beat about the bush, I meant *men* – who'd get me drunk in restaurants I couldn't afford and clubs I didn't know existed, and fuck me, or let me fuck them, I wasn't fussy. Not true – I was always discriminating; I just wasn't prejudiced. And, if the chance came, if we fucked each other, fucked together, and fell in love, well, I would be open-minded enough to consider that proposition, too. Though it would mostly be the sort that gets you killed, if Big Joe Turner is to be believed. 'Cherry Red', if you're wondering, JJ . . . which was also a very different – by which I mean truly bloody awful – Bee Gees song you've probably never heard and if I were you I'd keep it that way.

If I were you?

If I were you, JJ, I'd be dead, and –

By *fun* I meant that I was nearly thirty. We were nearly thirty. I wanted to eradicate the dark, damp over-crowded slums just as much as you did, to build the homes Nye Bevan promised. But I was nearly thirty and there had to be more to life than watching you underestimate your beautiful wife and get promoted every other year.

Diana has flopped into the armchair, as if settling in for the evening. ~Have you seen them? ~Seen what? Seen who? ~My spectacles. She means her reading glasses. They're here, on the table in front of me, where she put them after failing to read my aborted script. ~I got as far as Jamaica Road, she says. Why is she telling me this? ~I'd better leave it a while now.

We turned thirty the following year, 1961. I was getting old. You were very young. Young for the job you were pro- moted to. Assistant Director. We were not identical, but I felt I was getting younger again when Brian Wilmot asked if you were any relation. ~There can't be that many Jellicoes around? ~You'd be surprised, I said. (But he was right. We have not thrived.)

~Shall I make us a pot of tea? Diana asks, not moving from the armchair. I tell her I've written nothing more. She says I should just think of something nice, something positive, she says. How hard can it be? ~Positive? ~Cheerful. How hard? If only she knew. He *withdrew*. He refused to engage. He cultivated his garden. (Even if he didn't have a garden.) She said, You were at the wedding? ~I was the best man. ~There you go, then. Talk about that. Talk about their marriage. That's more important than bloody Rochester House.

Was it though? *I never loved, or hoped.* Was their marriage important? Oh, I don't mean to those who died. To Robert and Catherine Peters, to Elijah Johnson, to Rabia Leel, to Beth Williams and her children, Gwyneth and David – whose flat it was, the Williams', on the eighteenth floor, where the wall popped out and the collapse began. To the families who survived them. The parents who buried their children; the children – the Peters' children who had been staying with their grandparents that night – who buried their parents. (Burying your parents is the way of the world: but not, you might hope, at their age – or our age, as it happens, the age JJ and I were when our parents kicked the bucket.) Or even to the other families, the survivors, whether or not surviving caused them any later problems – psychologically, I mean: survivor guilt we might say now. (Did we say it then, in 1968, when, let's face it, it wasn't that long since the war and many of them had survived worse?) They'd have been evacuated, decanted, made homeless – again, many of them – just months after they'd moved to the future and got used to the lifts, to the views

34

and not having to get up in the dark to put a match to the fire, after they'd made new friends, established new routines, new routes to work, to church or to the mosque, found new shops, a new local on a Saturday night. They'd been thrown out again, scattered wherever JJ and the council could re-house all five hundred of them

Not all.

That's right: seven would cause no problem from that point of view. Or nine, in fact: the Peters' children remained with their grandparents on the Isle of Dogs and grew up fine, JJ told me, did well at a new school, and made new friends. He kept in touch, not in touch, but aware. He kept an eye on them, their progress. Eric was always good at drawing and became a draughtsman in an engineering firm, moved down to Thornton Heath, while his sister Jackie, who was pretty as a picture, got a job in Manze's despite not being Italian, and married a bank clerk who came in for eels, hoping to catch a glimpse of Charlie Richardson, who was on the run by then, and caught Jackie instead. And, after that, JJ didn't know how the story ended, he said, though he could guess and it was maybe not for the best. But surely it was no longer his responsibility? Not at that distance, that far removed?)

So, no. I don't imagine for a moment that the wedding of Beatrice and Jolyon Jellicoe, or even the years of undeniable love and affection and support and friendship they gave each other (until they didn't), was more important for any one of all those people than what happened at Rochester House in the early summer of 1968, much as it barely seemed to register with the rest of the world, lost in a barrage of news unlike any other, at least until now, the last twelve months, 2016 into 2017, summer again, June again, when history seems, again, to be speeding up.

But to JJ? Was it important to JJ?

Never loved, never hoped I never would.

To Diana, I say, Do you think so? ~I remember the wedding day, she says. It was lovely. *Is she mad? Does she not remember how it ended?* ~You looked identical, she said. ~We were. ~Of course you were. But in your suits. I don't know how Auntie Beatrice could tell you apart. This is not something I want to talk about. Now or at the funeral, so I say: He hadn't seen Bee since 1986. ~I know, but . . . still. ~What? ~It's still better than talking about Rochester House.

The trouble is, there's no real way to separate the two.

We turned thirty a couple of years after you married, when you were promoted, again. We were thirty and we were identical when Brian Wilmot asked if you were my brother and I said yes, you were. I wasn't ashamed. But I was not my brother's keeper, I said. Not for the last time. That wasn't what Brian wanted to know.

Were you ashamed of me?

Thirty pieces of silver, you said, and I told you I was holding out for thirty-two. You – we – only asked for decent homes, where old people could relax and families could raise their children in daylight, in warmth and space, where those children could be regularly bathed and sleep in their own bedrooms. For something better than we had known. Isn't that what we are all supposed to do? To demand a better world for those who come after us? I was just like you: a builder, a creator, a contributor. Your job was to clear slums and put people in new houses. Mine was to calculate and control the costs, whatever they built. As usual, when we had this conversation, Bee tried to mediate. We're none of us perfect, she said. ~Except you, I said. She laughed and JJ made a sour face.

We were at the Festival Hall again, I think. The bar. Gin for me and Bee and bottles of beer for George and JJ. It was 1962 and I had finally been accepted into the Royal Institute of Chartered Surveyors. I was getting on at Wilmots. I had a new friend and a TR3 in British Racing Green with a white cloth top I paid more to garage than I did to rent the double room in Bute Street. If I wasn't perfect I was pretty much as close as I would ever get. The concert was John Cage – my fault: by way of revenge, I imagine. Or to bamboozle George, the new friend. ~I try, Bee said, à propos of the music. I really try. JJ said it was degenerate; George said he wouldn't go that far. I knew he was only trying to keep the peace. Which was ironic, really, what with him being a soldier. I knew he wouldn't be my friend for very long. ~It *is*, JJ said. Degenerate. Under the table my hand squeezed George's thigh without my meaning to. He pushed it away. And he was right, of course. Throwing everything away for fun was one thing. This was just stupid. ~I'm all for the modern, JJ said. I'll happily tear down old stuff that doesn't work. You know I will. But you have to build up something in its place. Otherwise it's just childish, destruction for the fun of it. Anarchy. ~You sound like Dad, I said, and unfortunately it was true. Filling the silence, George said: You haven't introduced me to your father. At which JJ laughed, or snorted. ~Take no notice, George, I said. Our dad died in the war. ~And we both know what he'd have thought of you, don't we? I chose to assume JJ was talking about my class loyalty, not my other degeneracy. ~Me? I said. I'm a Chartered Surveyor. I have letters after my name. I build houses. ~For money. ~He was a communist, for pity's sake. He never said that we should work for free. ~You know what I mean. ~You mean working for a council that gives ratepayers' money to contractors to build homes for working

37

people is somehow more pure than working for the contractor who builds them?

Which is when Bee intervened. ~We all have a part to play, she said. And none of us is perfect. ~Except you, I said. *Have I said this already?* George volunteered to buy another round. ~I'm sorry about the Cage, I said. We could see Louis Jordan next week. At the Flamingo. With Snake-hips Johnson. Okay, they're second and third bill to Chris Barber, of all people – *because Barber was white; because he was British* – but, still. JJ said, The Flamingo's a dive. ~So what? In her continuing desire for peace, Bee said: Maybe. ~Maybe it's a dive? Or maybe you'll come?

It was in Lewisham. It was a dive.

To Diana I say: Have I already said this? ~I think so, Uncle Charlie. ~You weren't listening, were you? ~You say so many things. *So many things. Is that wrong?* ~Tomorrow, Uncle Charlie? Try to say just one thing. And try to make it about Uncle Jolyon, won't you? ~What else? ~I mean . . . Don't take this the wrong way, Uncle Charlie. Try not to talk about yourself.

I laugh. Diana might be a pain in the arse, but she's not stupid. ~Then I'll have to talk about Rochester House. She shakes her head. ~That's always just as much about you. *Not stupid at all.* ~What else is there? ~Talk about what he loved. Talk about the art and theatre and music he enjoyed. ~I could. ~You could. ~But it would all be bollocks, and – *it would.* He loved work and he loved Bee. Nothing wrong with that, but the rest was all her doing, and she won't be there. The truth is Rochester House was the biggest thing in JJ's life, even after we tore it down. It might have stopped, then. But it didn't, and that was thirty years ago. I can't talk about a void.

She tried. I know she tried. She was so proud of him, then.

When they married. When he was promoted. And later, in 1966, when he was promoted again. Housing Director. The youngest in London. That had to count for something. I told him he'd be earning more than me. He said it wasn't about the money. And it wasn't. Not for him. And not for me. It really wasn't.

It wasn't the status, either. The previous Director was some old duffer who'd been there since the place was built, who'd seen off the politicians, seen off the Town Clerk, to occupy the best room in the whole town hall. JJ barely noticed. You could only get to it through an antechamber full of secretaries. Inside, you'd find space enough to swing the biggest cat you could drum up, if it hadn't been for all the furniture. The windows were covered with blackout-grade curtains that turned the brightest day into sepulchral gloom, through which you could just about make out the bookcases and filing cabinets, the defensive enfilades of heavy, leather-backed armchairs around a meeting table big enough to land a helicopter on, all blocking your route towards the old Director's desk – a vast, boat-shaped expanse of polished walnut generally unencumbered by a single sheet of paper. When JJ inherited the office, he changed nothing, although the desk gradually disappeared beneath tottering piles of draft reports, annotated committee papers and half-read periodicals. He was too busy to worry about his working environment, he said. *The youngest Housing Director in London.* And the best, Bee always said, and who was I to disagree? He was thirty-five years old. Thirty-five, when the old duffer retired, or died. Died probably. Discovered rotting amongst the walnut furniture after a couple of weeks of nobody noticing he wasn't there, I shouldn't wonder. It would have been the smell that alerted them in the end, or the flies. Of course it wasn't really like that, Diana. What do you think this is? The point was, he – JJ – was only thirty-five. He was the deputy who'd been running the show for a few years anyway. The one Brian Wilmot had heard of. The one the councillors came to when they saw the high-rise blocks going up across the river. Despite everything we've done, they told him, and he told me, despite all that, there's still ten thousand families in this borough living in houses we condemned more than a decade ago. Privies out the back. No baths. No hot water, half of them. Hovels. It's a fucking crime, they said, and – *it was, though not the only one* – it was a fucking crime, and – none of it was news to him, or me. It was the water we swam in. Why we did what we did. To right the wrongs, to fight the fight, to build the new Jerusalem.

It wasn't about the money. Not when Brian Wilmot said: *It's time.* It was about the fun. Five years already I'd been at Wilmots.

A fucking crime.

About time.

T. Dan Smith wasn't in jail, then. Poulson wasn't Poulson. I mean, he was, of course, we just didn't know it. He was John Poulson, architect. Sort of. Owner of the largest architectural practice in England, anyway: he was never an actual architect. What he wasn't, then, was Poulson the bankrupt fraudster connected to everyone all the way up to the Cabinet. To what's his name? Reggie. Not Kray, though you never knew, really. Maudlin. Not Maudlin: *Maudling.* Sir Reginald Maudling. Threatened to sue everyone in sight, then died.

How come I remember that? *Heath, Wilson, Douglas-Home.*

I'd worked on a couple of dozen blocks around the country. I'd spent miserable times in Portsmouth and Wolverhampton, which wasn't exactly what I'd had in mind that day on the Euston Road when I said I was skipping out of the council.

Thirty pieces of silver, you said. I hadn't bargained on the flea-ridden digs in Coventry, though. Or weeks in Lancashire mill towns where the swinging 60s never really swung. But the fact was there were Housing Committee chairmen all over the country snapping up high-rise blocks like bags of sweeties. JJ's political bosses would be no different, Brian said. It was time to bring things closer to home. Have a word with Peter.

Diana says, Who's Peter? ~Did I say that aloud? She is putting her coat back on. Will the traffic have cleared by now? Surely it's too early, still? ~You said: Have a word with Peter. Peter was Piotr Sakowicz was Peter Sack. Everyone knew Peter. Or rather, Peter knew everyone. ~I must have been daydreaming.

Where would Peter Sack be now? The House of Lords, most likely, if he's alive. No. I'd have heard. If he's alive, he must be knocking on a hundred.

Ninety-six.

He'd be ninety-six – the same as Angela.

It was always hard to believe that he was only ten years older than us. Fighter pilot in the war, Brian told me. Flew a Hurricane in 303 Squadron, he said. Shot down five Jerry planes in a single day. ~Really? ~Really – *don't say "really"* – he's got the gong to show for it, not that he does. Too much class. Lives in a seventeenth-century sandstone manor house somewhere in Gloucestershire. When he isn't at his club. Or Chequers.

Brian Wilmot had been in the RAF, too. So had I, come to that. Though in my case it was national service and I never saw the inside of a plane. Even when they shipped us out to Malaya they . . . shipped us. Four weeks in a boat with a couple of hundred bored aircraftmen certainly beat basic training. (Didn't I ever want to fly, Bee once asked. Was she mad? I said. Far too fucking dangerous.) Malaya was an infantry war. Ambushes. Burning out jungle villages and such. There was pretty much nothing for the RAF to do. I'd signed up to get it over with, but national service was where I first discovered the joy of idleness, first glimpsed the lack of correlation between effort and reward, an epiphany that subsequent years of night school never quite snuffed out. Tony – Angela's Tony – would have enjoyed national service, I remember thinking, if he hadn't manufactured flat feet to keep out of the war. He'd have been good at it.

Brian said: Peter has fingers in a lot of pies, if you follow my drift. He's been a friend of Wilmots since the start. It would be good for you to meet him. I thought I was something then. I thought: this is why I left the council. I didn't think: why me? Perhaps I thought that was obvious.

Brian took me to a party in a tall, narrow London terrace where the window glass had been gently slumping toward the bottom of the panes since seventeen-oh-something. Denis Healey was there, arguing loudly with Harold Evans about aircraft carriers. Rita Tushingham spat martini olive stones at Peter Cook, who was impersonating the new Defence Secretary behind his back, using rolled-up napkins in place of bushy eyebrows. Muriel Spark, in a pale pink twinset, picked up the stones and arranged them neatly in a saucer while ignoring Basil Spence's attempts to chat her up.

Bee didn't believe a word of it. JJ said: Basil Spence? Now I know you're lying, but I wasn't. Not about Spence.

Piotr Sakowicz was in a quiet room, upstairs from the main party, when Brian and I found him seated with two other men in wing-backed armchairs around an empty fireplace. ~Peter, Brian said, having waited for them to finish what they were saying. ~Brian! How the devil are you? He sprang

42

from his chair, hand outstretched. You know David? And Jeremy? The three men nodded to each other. ~And who is this? Brian introduced me, and we shook hands. Peter was tiny. Shorter even than me, and about half my weight. His hair and eyebrows were pale, the colour and weight of froth on beer. I thought he looked more like a spy than a property developer, then thought that was ridiculous. Philby had looked like the civil servant he was. If spies looked like spies they wouldn't be much good at their job. His handshake was firm and lasted just long enough to suggest that he really was pleased to meet me. He asked how long I'd been at Wilmots and what it was I did for Brian there. ~A couple of years, I said. (I rounded down, not wanting to sound like I'd been stuck in the slow lane. If Peter was such a friend of the firm, why hadn't I been introduced before?) I'm a QS, I said. ~Really? Brian should have introduced you sooner. Please, fetch over a chair. And, when Brian and I had joined the semi-circle, Piotr Sakowicz, with the air of including us in the conversation we had interrupted, asked if I knew Dick Crossman. Who had just been appointed Housing Minister.

This must have been a couple of years earlier. Before Brian said it was time. It must have been '64.

I remember this stuff. I do. I remember it all. You just can't expect me to keep it in the right order. *Wilson, Douglas-Home, Macmillan, Eden, Churchill, Atlee.* Prime Ministers are easy. It's the other stuff. Stuff I can picture happening, hear the words. But can I be sure they happened before or after other pictures, other words?

~People say he's difficult, Peter continued before I could say anything too stupid. But I have to say we've always got on perfectly well. Then he asked me about myself, my family. If we were related to Lord Jellicoe, who'd been a defence minister before the recent election? He showed no disappointment when I said we weren't. He commiserated the loss of my parents and seemed genuinely tickled by the notion of twin boys, orphaned by the Luftwaffe, who'd grown up wanting to rebuild the city beneath which our parents had been buried. ~Like Romulus and Remus, the one called David – or possibly Jeremy – said. ~Not quite, I hope, said Peter, smiling at me. I trust Mr. Jellicoe is not going to kill his brother. I said I hadn't planned to. They laughed. We laughed. Brian and I left.

I would be back in Plymouth in the morning, and Piotr Sakowicz would have forgotten all about me. But for the moment I felt that I was made. I was wrong. Peter Sack never forgot a thing.

Now, to Diana, I say: I must have been daydreaming. I say, Peter was a friend. ~Of Uncle Jolyon's? ~Not exactly. Diana sighs, as only Diana can. Her sigh means that I am being difficult, again. But am I? Vague, perhaps, but that was Peter, in a way. What had I meant by "not exactly"? I'm not sure they ever even met. But Peter was everybody's friend, whether they knew it or not. Peter helped me; I helped JJ.

The second time we met, he asked me about Plymouth. At his suggestion, we were in a restaurant in Greek Street. He had advised me against the hake. Today is Monday, he said. That fish will have spent all weekend staring at the chef through ever-duller eyes. How did it go, he asked, meaning Plymouth.

It had been three months. I thought my memory was good, but even I was struggling to make the connection. ~When we met, he said, you were going to have to get up early to catch a morning train to Plymouth. I was brash enough to ask how on earth he had remembered such mundane details. ~I find it helps, he said, to be interested in other people. He smiled, pleasantly. ~Honestly? I said. Plymouth's a dump. Bombed to buggery. I watched his eyes when I said "buggery", but there was nothing to see. ~Which means there will be plenty of opportunity, I said. ~It's a very ill wind? I nodded. ~And what is Wilmots' share of this particular silver lining? ~You're mixing your metaphors, I said. He smiled again, nodding in approval. I felt as though I'd passed a test.

He must surely have been aware of Wilmots' interest from Brian. In any case, it was no secret. ~A small estate, I said. A couple of high-rise blocks, some lower stuff. They want us to chuck in a tenants' hall for free. He asked if I knew Councillor Cox. I said I'd been trying to meet him. Peter nodded again. I got the feeling that the next time I was in Plymouth my contact, who had always been politely unhelpful, might just suggest I meet the councillor after all.

The cherry soup arrived, which at least allowed a decent pause before Peter asked how my brother was getting on. ~You're twins, you said? You and Jolyon? I found myself explaining – justifying – your ridiculous name. ~Dad said it was his turn to choose: Mum had chosen Angela, for our sister. He wanted to call us Karl and Joseph. ~He was a Stalinist? ~It was 1931. He was a communist. Mum wasn't. She said all right, at least it wasn't Vladimir, so he let her go to the registrar while he was at work. Angela says the look on Dad's face when she told him what she'd done made it almost worth having a brother called Jolyon. Mum said she thought it had a nice ring. Jolyon Jellicoe. She said Dad should stop moaning, they could always call him Joe, just the same. But we never did. It was Mum's little victory, but he was only ever Jolyon to her, JJ to the rest of us. ~And you? What did they call you?

45

They called me Charlie, I thought. That was obvious. But I had a feeling it wasn't what Piotr meant.

Should I talk about Bee? Tomorrow? About your life together, like Diana says? Wouldn't that just cause more trouble than Rochester House? It's not a story that ends well, after all. But you loved her, didn't you? She loved you. That's surely worth a mention?

~Do you think there's any chance that she'll be there? ~Who? *Who, she says* ~Beatrice. Diana shrugs, says nothing. ~Would you? I ask, knowing it's an unfair question. Diana is seventy-five; she has never married. Never, as far as I know, come close. But what do I know? I suppose I could ask her. *Diana, have you ever been engaged?* She has, in fact, I know she has, although she never told us. So I can't ask. It would cause her pain. Besides, what business is it of mine? I'm not the marrying kind. Even if now – thanks to David Cameron, of all people – I could. In theory.

It wasn't the law that stopped me marrying, any more than it stopped me having sex before 1967. We were thirty-six by then. Did you imagine I was a virgin, JJ? Did you imagine what George and I got up to? (Bee did. She asked me once: which of us was the lady? I said it wasn't like that. We weren't dancing. ~What then? ~Fucking, Bee. We were fucking. ~Yes, but . . . ? She was genuinely curious.) Still – marrying? Staying married? The family record is patchy, at best. There's Mum and Dad, of course – blown apart together. Angela and Tony lasted longer than anyone could believe, but they weren't exactly role models, were they? Frances and Philip. My sweet Frances, *who was not loved, nor loved had been* – except by me: Philip never was your match. Diana and I, eternal spinsters. You didn't do so badly, JJ.

And then there's Dougie, last of the Jellicoe line. Another confirmed bachelor, as we used to say – but perhaps you'll marry now, Dougie? It's not too late. You'll not. You're a boy after my own selfish heart, and I love you for it.

Christ. If I'm going to get this maudlin sober, I might as well drink after all.

I met Peter every few months: in restaurants and bars, for the most part, occasionally at private parties. If he had an office, I never saw it. If he had a job, he never mentioned it, and neither did any of the countless acquaintances he introduced me to, directly or indirectly. Peter Sack knew everybody, and wanted everybody to know each other.

It helps, he said, to be interested in other people.

I'd nod, but –

My job changed, then, the nature of it changed, after Peter. I saw more of Brian. I spent less time on building sites, more in town halls, and in restaurants and nightclubs. For work, I mean. I was a QS. I became less sure I knew what I was doing, even as it seemed my career was blossoming. I was heading in exactly the direction I had hoped, and I had no idea what I was doing. This is no defence. I'm not pleading ignorance. I just mean my work became less specific, less technical, less professional. More fun.

I saw less of JJ, for a while, less of Bee.

I was busy, and not just with work. George had gone the way of all Georges, but there were others. I moved out of Bute Street, with a twinge of regret. We all love a touch of shabbiness, don't we? At least in retrospect. I bought a flat in Chelsea Square. (No, really: I did. Despite the book.) This was 1965, when such a thing was possible, but it was still a bone of contention, wasn't it, JJ? Not Chelsea in particular.

Just buying was enough. Buying a flat. You thought it was of a piece with working for Wilmots, and perhaps you weren't wrong, at that. You said I would never send my children to private schools. I said that wasn't likely to be an issue, was it? ~You wouldn't pay for private doctors. ~I wouldn't. It's true. (Especially now, when I have more doctors than friends.) ~So why would you own a house? ~I have to live somewhere. ~Even K&C are building now, you said. And it was true: they were. But I doubt they'd have rented a flat to me: a single man of criminal proclivities, possessed of a more than adequate income. You said your council would. ~I'm shocked! I said. Shocked. Is that quite ethical? I may have winked.

But work kept me busy, too. Kept me for the most part out of JJ's way. I stayed in better hotels, but still spent half my life in Coventry, or Liverpool or Southampton or – God help me – Aberdeen. The concrete boom was on. High-rise blocks were sprouting all around us, like mushrooms after rain. I could – I did – argue brutalism and Bauhaus with the best of them, but that wasn't the job. The job was getting stuff done. That's what Brian said. Before the war, Walter Gropius had built a lovely school in the Fens and a house in Chelsea. One house. (Not my house, sadly. Wilmots wasn't paying that well.) In twenty years since the end of the war, we still hadn't sorted out the slums. Twenty years. We'd built the NHS. We'd whitewashed rock'n'roll and sold it back to the Yanks. But we still had families living in one room without running water. It was a fucking disgrace. It truly was. Dad would have been spinning in his grave, if there'd been enough of him left to bury.

Art schmart, as Dad's old boss, Manny Levinson, probably never said. Fuck art.

It's true that Basil Spence – God bless him, as He surely

did after Coventry Cathedral – had just finished the glorious Queen Elizabeth Square in Glasgow. Like a great ship in sail, he said, and it must have been one ginormous fucking boat he had in mind. But even so, it was only four hundred flats. One part of one development – Hutchesontown-Gorbals C – in one city. Construction alone took five years. Five years. His builders mixed their own concrete, on site, and poured it into massive shuttered moulds they'd built themselves. Like the South Bank: building as sculpture. Beautiful, in its way, I'm not denying. But slow. A craft, not an industry, at a time when Double Diamond was really taking off. When we had a world to build. In the white heat of the technological revolution, who could afford to wait? In the time it took Spence just to lay foundations, Wimpey chucked up three twenty-storey blocks just down the road, and housed as many people as would – eventually – live in the Queenies. In the five years it took Spence to finish, Wilmots built thirty estates – not blocks, *estates* – even if nobody who lived there could ever name the architect. So what? They had bathrooms and indoor toilets and bedrooms for the nippers and central heating. And I'd had a hand in maybe half of those. So who was right? Spence, of course. Nothing was too good for the working classes. But Glasgow council blew up Queen Elizabeth Square in 1993. Seven years after we demolished the Rochester.

So who was right?

What the Danes brought us – long before they brought us fizzy lager – was modern modernism. Industrialized. Systematized, replicable, cheap and easy. A system of pre-fabricated concrete slabs you could practically put together with an Allen key, like flat-pack furniture. Except without the joints. A triumph of convenience over soul. Like Brecht said, bread before poetry.

JJ had his doubts, I'll give him that.

~What? – *Christ. Is she still here?* ~I thought you'd left. ~Don't be silly, Uncle Charlie. You just asked me to get you a drink. It's right there. On the table beside you.

I check, and she's not lying. A Duralex tumbler with half an inch of brandy. I'll spend good money – is there any other kind? – on alcohol, but I'm not overly fussed about glassware. ~What did Uncle JJ have doubts about? I might as well tell her. She's asked for it. ~Large Panel System building. Her demeanour, which had been bright, if only for effect, collapses. She looks as if she has been reminded of some arduous chore she had succeeded in pushing from her mind. ~Oh, that, she says. ~He asked to meet the Danes himself. Diana sighs. Again. ~Uncle Charlie, you know that saying: it's your funeral? Well, it's not. It's really not.

I will pretend I don't know what she means.

Brian was delighted when I told him. Peter suggested we fly him over to meet a friend of his in Copenhagen. But JJ wasn't having any of it. ~Go on, I said. It'll be fun. ~I'm going nowhere on your expense account. ~Then pay for yourself. Or get the council to. It's work. We'll save you millions, so the ratepayers can afford it. But he said: The Danes can come here. I'd never tried to sell JJ anything before. Not directly. Brian had never asked me to.

To Diana I say, He'd just been promoted again. To Director. ~At thirty-five, she says. I know. The youngest in London – you can say that.

That's what we always said. Because it was true. Half true. *Is that still true?* The point is he *was* the youngest Housing Director in London, but the profession had only just been invented. There were architects, there were planners, there were managers of building works departments. Surveyors, of course.

Treasurers collected rent. Then there was social work: a different field, entirely. But it all started to come together, and people - people like JJ - started thinking about the families in the houses as much as the houses themselves, at the same time as the houses. As if local government had finally caught up with Octavia Hill. I say, His old boss had been the Borough Architect. ~So what? ~You're right. It's not important. The point is, though, Diana, my love, that when his old boss died, the councillors had choices. They didn't need to appoint this whippersnapper. There were more established men around whose noses they were putting out of joint. But they gave him the job because they trusted him. ~And? ~And he had to repay that trust. And Brian had said: it's time.

It was about time.

When JJ was promoted, Bee was thrilled. Proud as punch. She arranged a party. A joint birthday/promotion/housewarming party, she said. We haven't seen much of you lately, Charlie. They'd moved onto one of the new estates JJ managed. Two bedrooms plus a living room bigger than our old house in Dennett's Road. The flat was on the top floor - the fourteenth - facing west, with a view back up the river and over the City. ~I pay rent, JJ said, unprompted, when Bee invited me over to help plan the party. ~Of course you do. ~We allocated the flats randomly, he said. We all came here, all the new tenants, came to the hall and picked a set of keys out of a big bowl. ~Of course you did, I said. ~No one knew what they were getting.

~So can I invite Brian? I asked, and JJ said: Don't you fucking dare. ~Why not? Bee said. We're both proud of you. We want to show you off. She meant JJ. At least I assumed she did. I said, It's my birthday, too. ~You can bring George. ~That's very big of you, JJ. But George is history. ~You can bring a friend. ~Just the one? ~You know what I mean. I did, but I wasn't going to let that distract us. ~What are you afraid of? It took a while for JJ to answer, but Bee and I both waited. ~It's a private party, he said eventually. Not a trade fair.

Truth was, if it had been up to you, there'd have been no party at all, would there, JJ? But it wasn't, and the event gathered a momentum of its own. Story of your life, eh?

It was originally going to be in the new flat, the flat on the estate he'd just built, with no help at all from Wilmots. But Bee soon realized, what with our family and her friends and all the neighbours and JJ's colleagues – and she couldn't *not* invite the local ward councillors, and the Leader and the Chairman of the Housing Committee, it would have been rude – she realized that big as the new living room was, it wasn't going to do. So she hired the tenants' hall – yes, she sighed, when JJ objected, yes she'd make sure we paid – and spent hours making banners and doing stuff with crepe paper to disguise the fact that it was a cheerless municipal barn, even if the paint was fresh. She even got her class in on the act, although she didn't tell JJ that until the night itself, when it was too late for him to object, or to do anything other than be polite to the children's parents when they said how much they'd enjoyed it and what a wonderful teacher his wife was.

I took Piotr. Peter. Everybody's friend. I told him not to expect too much. He said he wouldn't miss it for the world. And, allowing for hyperbole, he meant it. This was not an occasion he would want to miss. I advised him to drink a glass or two of something decent before he came. I wasn't sure how far, despite my encouragement, Bee's budget would run. He offered to pick me up and drive us over. By which, it turned out, he meant: have us driven over, stopping off on the way for cocktails at the Savoy. I tried not to embarrass myself. Driving east, leaving the City behind and crossing Tower Bridge, I fell silent. Peter watched me watch the terraces slide by, along with the cafés and the shops – there was Tomas' – from the back seat of his Jaguar. ~Home again, home again? he said and I nodded. ~Sarf London, me, mate. He laughed. ~Peckham's own Dick Van Dyck, he said. Mate was a word I'd used a lot in the RAF, and on the building sites. Peter was not a mate; he was a friend. ~Never outgrow your roots, he said. I had to direct his driver the last half mile and on to JJ's estate. I said I hadn't seen *Mary Poppins*, but I was lying. Of course I had.

I pointed out JJ's block, and the driver parked right in front of it. There was no shortage of space. Peter said, Where is everybody? ~They don't need to drive. They all live here, or hereabouts. That wasn't quite true, either. I could see Tony's powder blue Ford Consul parked over by the tenants' hall. Diana would be coming by bus. Peter invited his driver to come in with us, but he peered dubiously around the estate before declaring that he would prefer to stay with the car.

Angela was near the door when we entered, looking as though she'd already necked a couple of bottles of Hirondelle. My sister, I whispered to Peter, who insisted I introduce him. ~Tony's over there somewhere, she said, waving a hand broadly – the hand not holding a glass, the one pinching a cigarette between the first and second fingers while the others wedged the packet against her palm – indicating the other end of the hall. With Frances, she added.

I had little choice but to abandon Peter and thread my way through an already dense crowd. I recognized a few of JJ's colleagues. They were mostly men – planners, architects, housing managers, a couple of councillors. They wore suits. Most of them wore ties. I looked out for the Leader, but he didn't seem to be there. Not yet. The women were younger, for the most part, and more colourful in bright short dresses.

53

Only the occasional twinset. No one was dancing to the music that trickled feebly from the record player set up on a wooden chair in one corner of the hall. Connie Francis. No wonder no one was dancing. I would have to sort that out later.

Tony was standing by a line of crepe-covered trestle tables. One end was all plates of sandwiches and bowls of crisps; the other, drinks. Cans of Long Life had been stacked into a pretty reasonable simulacrum of the new estate around us. Tony spotted me and waved. ~JJ! Have a beer. It is JJ, isn't it? He liked to pretend he still couldn't tell us apart. Or perhaps he couldn't. He reached out and pulled a can from about half way up what would be Bee and JJ's block. The tower wobbled, then fell, taking its neighbours down with it. There was a loud clattering as the cans cascaded onto the low-rise stacks around them and bounced onto the floor. One burst, spraying our ankles with foam. ~Had to happen, Tony said. It was a stupid idea, putting them up like that in the first place.

People shrank rapidly away from us, from the spreading pool of beer. Frances, improbably, appeared to clear it up. Nineteen, blonde as straw to Diana's ginger, in a sheath dress and carrying a mop, with a smile for her uncle that lit the place up like an ack-ack searchlight, she looked like perfect wartime propaganda. I hugged her. ~My favourite niece, I said. ~You shouldn't say that, Uncle Charlie. Which of course was when I spotted Diana over her shoulder. Christ. Where had she sprung from?

The fact is, Frances *was* my favourite niece. Still is. I can't help it. They both know it. In Herefordshire, during the war, we spared a couple of kittens from the sack. Both beautiful, if you like kittens. As they grew up, one stayed beautiful, grew proud, let you stroke her on her own terms, and then purred like a barrel rolling down a cellar ramp. The other would cringe every time you moved and still get under your feet and make you want to drop kick her over the barn. No rhyme or reason to it, I could see. Diana was the second kitten, is what I'm saying. Angela put them both through secretarial school. Diana worked at the London Hospital, typing medical records. Frances had just got a job at the BBC.

She said: Uncle Charlie, I want you to meet Philip. ~I can't keep up. Who's Philip? ~Philip, said Tony, butting in sourly, is my future son-in-law. I swear Frances actually blushed. ~Don't be silly, Dad. We've only just met. ~Well, I've a friend I want you to meet, too, I said, then wondered why. What good would come of introducing Peter to any of my family? Other than JJ, of course. That was why he was here, the way it worked. The way Peter worked, even when he wasn't working. And it might help Frances. Or Frances' young man. You never knew.

~So, this Philip. What's he like, then?

Tall and dark and handsome, Diana said. ~Really? Then I definitely want to meet him. ~Hands off, Frances said. He's mine. ~And what does he do, this Philip? ~He's a policeman. (Ah. That would account for the expression on Tony's face.) ~Training to be a detective. I didn't say: then Peter will definitely want to meet him. Instead, I said: Has anyone seen my brother? The man of the hour? No one had.

I poured myself a glass of wine, looked at the bottle. Bulgarian. Maybe not as bad as that made it sound. The Bulgarians invented wine.

Someone changed the record. And there it was again. Dave Bastard Brubeck. There's nothing wrong with 'Take Five', JJ had said, another time, when I'd complained once before. More than once, I dare say. ~Just because everybody likes it, he said. ~You can't dance in five-four, I said, and the rest of the album's worse: nine-seven, for fuck sake. Bee said, You can't dance to John Cage, either, which I probably deserved. At a party, though, I wanted to dance. Or at least for there to be the possibility of dancing.

I poured Frances a glass of Bulgarian red, then took her free hand in mine and led her over to the record player. ~Let's find something for the young people, I said, and you can tell me all about your Philip. I rejected the Beatles in favour of the Troggs. ~How come this is here? ~I brought it, Frances said, to show you. Which was one reason why I loved the girl. ~It was a present from someone at work. ~And what did Philip think of that? Frances laughed. ~He didn't mind, she said. I nodded. ~He sounds a decent sort. Where is he? ~Helping Auntie Bee out in the kitchen. ~Better and better. I think it's time I met this paragon.

The tenants' hall had a kitchen you could have used to run a fair-sized restaurant, but Philip wasn't in it. Bee was slicing fruit with a knife that looked like something you might see strapped to a scuba diver's thigh. We kissed. Both cheeks. Not something everybody did in 1966. Not with their in-laws, anyway.

Happy Birthday, she said. That's right. It was my birthday, too. ~Thanks. Where's JJ? At the same time, Frances said, Where's Philip? Bee laughed. ~Philip's chucking rubbish in the bins outside. I left JJ in the flat, getting ready. Has he not come down yet? I said: Getting ready? What's he doing? Combing his suit? Bee shrugged. ~Take this, she said, handing Frances a platter of chopped up pineapple and cheese. ~He's not preparing a speech, is he? Bee shrugged again. ~Oh god. He is, isn't he? Bee said: Weren't you going to say a few words? ~Of course. That's different.

It was different. *Because?* Because whatever JJ's strengths

– and I've always been prepared to admit he has strengths – a way with words has never been among them. He'd talk about slums, for pity's sake. About the lack of light and indoor plumbing. He'd talk about concrete and streets in the sky. Which might be just about excusable – it wasn't *just* a birthday party, after all – but he'd manage to be dull about it. He would talk earnestly, and at length, with not a word about himself.

The family looked to me on such occasions. On any occasion, really. Like tomorrow. Even if I weren't the oldest Jellicoe standing. I could be trusted to keep it light, and brief. *So why am I struggling now? Why won't Diana trust me?* A few words. Light. And brief. ~You're right, I say. I'll keep it light. ~It's a funeral, Uncle Charlie. I'm not sure 'light' is what you're after. *See? Not dumb.* ~All right. Brief. ~Good. ~The best jokes are all about death, anyway.

Angela came into the kitchen. The hubbub of music and voices rose as she pushed open the stainless steel-plated doors, subsided again as they swung shut behind her. To Bee she said: You're going to need another case of that white wine. To me, she said: Your friend Peter is a charmer. ~Isn't he? ~A bit old for you, though, don't you think? ~He's the same age as you, Angela. ~That's what I mean. I'm practically your mum.

The fact was, he wasn't old for me. In those days I had two types of friends. The Georges were mostly younger, good-looking, not always very bright. The others were older – older than me, certainly, but older even than Peter, sometimes, too. Also good-looking, most of the time. And rich. Or richer than me, which was just as good. But I didn't usually introduce the older ones to the Jellicoe clan.

I said Peter wasn't that kind of friend. ~No? Are you sure? He likes you. ~He likes everybody. (Which wasn't true. Peter was *polite* to everybody. There's a difference.) ~Perhaps.

I realized I hadn't seen him since we'd arrived, had not introduced him to anyone other than Angela. I asked her what she'd done with him. She waved an empty glass airily. ~Oh, left him talking to some boring man with an orange face and sideburns. I relaxed. The sideburns would belong to Cllr Simpson, Chairman of the Housing Committee. Piotr Sakowicz did not need any help from me.

Finally, JJ arrived - shiny-faced and hair neatly parted - sidling through the back door into the kitchen, trailing a handsome tall young man I guessed must be Philip. Bee hugged and kissed JJ. I hugged him too, somewhat to his surprise. In the process I confirmed my worst suspicions. There, in his jacket pocket, were at least a dozen pages torn from a notebook. I marched him straight out of the kitchen and into the main hall, delegating Frances to turn the music off. Before JJ could open his mouth, I sprang nimbly onto one of the trestle tables, scattering a stack of empty beer cans to the floor.

I faced the crowd. I opened my mouth.

I talked about JJ's youth - our youth - and the future. I talked about concrete and tower blocks. I spotted and flattered the Leader of the Council; I proposed a toast to JJ. I did it all in ninety seconds and got at least three decent laughs.

Tomorrow will be fine.

This morning I went for a walk in the park.

Yesterday morning. By tomorrow it will be yesterday. Does it matter? Verisimilitude is not the effect I'm after here. But, still. I start again, aloud:

Yesterday morning I went for a walk in the park.

[Pause.]

I know what you're thinking, I continue. *You're thinking*

58

why – how? – does a man with a mobility scooter, a Rollator and a knobkerrie take a stroll around his local park? Especially a park that – if you know my corner of south London, and JJ's, the corner where we were born – sits on top of a hill? And lacks a single level pathway. Shouldn't I content myself with a trip to the local shop for a newspaper and a pint of semi-skimmed? Should I not, when the electronic gates roll back (no Baldie now, just a key-code entry pad) turn my scooter to the right, not the left, keep on the flat and enjoy all the benefits the Queen's Road has to offer? We have a Tesco Metro these days, after all. A bakery-cum-café has opened in the railway arches. There is chicken – jerk and southern-fried – and also, lately, sourdough pizza and craft beer. Peckham isn't what it used to be. It never was.

I'll have to cut this back. Diana's right: it's not my funeral. All the same, Peckham's changed. There are fewer black faces for a start. Or rather: more white ones. Not more than 1935, when this place opened; but more than there were twenty-five years ago, when I moved back. They are often young, these whites. I haven't conducted a census, but I'd say my neighbours in the Centre are more likely to be white than Peckham as a whole. (Though there's Mrs. Vega of course.) Which is not at all why I am here. They're more likely to be single, too, or at least not to have children. Which is a turn-up. When this place was really the home of the Peckham Experiment, you had to be a family, or they wouldn't let you in. Membership was by family. The place was here to prove that health was not just the absence of disease, but the opportunity to grow. And growth could only occur, un-stunted, in the context of the family: man plus woman plus children. The Biologists who ran the place believed the family was the complete human organism: only through the birth and growth of this collective organism could individuals realize their potential maturity. It was a radical utopia. One where it was simply not possible to be homosexual and healthy. And where everyone was white.

It was an experiment, all right.

We were four in 1935, JJ and I. We were only eight when the Ministry of War requisitioned the place. It wasn't something we talked about. There was table tennis, swimming, the gym. And dancing. Dance classes – self-organized, no teachers – and every Saturday night a social dance, the men in their best suits and ties, the women in tea dresses, for the most part. And you could dance, or not dance. You could just watch, and no one minded. Everybody cared, and no one minded. That's what they said. And after the war we never returned.

I returned. I live here now: not just for the beauty of the building's architecture, which has survived its conversion into flats; not because the value of those flats has rocketed over the years; and certainly not because their residents are mostly white, although these facts may be inter-related; but because I could not come here then, when the war ended and Dennett's Road – our end of Dennett's Road – had been obliterated. I am, when you get down to it, an old and sentimental fool.

Light; and brief.

Where was I? Walking in the park. Preparing to. The fact is that I'm not content to limit myself, to circumscribe my experience any more than absolutely bloody necessary. So, when the gates close themselves behind me, I do not always turn my scooter to the right, towards Queen's Road and the shops. This morning – yesterday morning – as I often do on fine mornings, I turned left. At the top of the road, by the church that wasn't there when we were growing up, I turned left again, and then almost immediately right, edging out between the parked cars and waiting for the traffic to pass before I crossed the road. Sometimes, too, when it is not fine. When it is cloudy and cool, or even damp, provided it is not actually raining. Not of course, when it is icy. At my age you have to be realistic, and I am not convinced the Easy Rider could handle an icy slope. To be sliding downhill, backwards, all traction lost, would be ignominious, however little real danger there might be. Another left-right dogleg, this time crossing a much busier, more difficult road, and then the long slow curving ascent begins. Park outside the shop to pick up a newspaper on the way. I may wish to sit in the early summer sunshine and read. There is an election on after all. I should keep up. Not that it will change my vote. The posters in the windows on these streets - where there are posters - are all red. Turn left past the pub - later, perhaps: it is only ten a.m. - and cross at the sleeping policeman - does anyone still call them that? I prefer it to the sniggering schoolboy connotations of "speed hump" - to reach bottom corner of the park. Attached to the gate, a metal plate details a local byelaw that prohibits bicycles and dogs.

I could drive the Easy Rider into the park - it is not a bicycle, and no one could object - but I don't. I pull up at the iron fence beside the gate and slowly, never letting go, swivel the seat to my left, put both feet on the pavement simultaneously and haul myself upright. As upright as I ever get these days. I take the newspaper from the basket, roll it up, and, awkwardly, shove it in my jacket pocket. I unfasten my stick from its Velcro loops, grasp its smooth, familiar knob, and I am good to go.

The path at this point is particularly steep. Curled over my stick like a question mark, I make my way a few inches at a time towards the first bench, twenty yards away or so. This may take a quarter of an hour. Once at the bench, I will rest for five or ten minutes before pressing on towards the summit of the hill, from which the prospect to the north and west offers a view of the city at least as good as that from Bee and JJ's old flat in Rochester House. I will stop at a second bench before I reach it. There is nowhere to sit at the summit. There's not even a path and I will have to make my way across muddy grass. On weekend mornings, particularly in summer, the ground is littered with cigarette butts, empty bottles and small hard shiny gas canisters like miniature artillery shells: this is a popular spot for young people to sit and watch the sun go down – if not, I suspect, come up. In winter, even when it is not actually raining, the ground is frequently too soft for my stick and I risk becoming marooned.

At the second bench I pull the newspaper from my pocket. Khuram Butt – one of the three men who drove their van towards the crowds on London Bridge, before attacking them with knives and being shot dead by police – was known to the security services and had even appeared on a Channel 4 documentary last year waving an ISIS flag. Jeremy Corbyn has denied being "soft on terror" and described as "utterly ridiculous and offensive" the Prime Minister's attempt to portray him as a threat. *May, Cameron, Brown, Blair.* And tomorrow? May again? We'll see. Tomorrow night, once JJ is safely incinerated, we'll see.

I could probably drive my scooter right up here to the top, at least in drier weather. But I don't. I leave it at the gate and creep and haul my way up for the same reason that I continue to live in a flat with a spiral staircase. Because I still can. Just. Am I not human? If you prick me do I not stab you in the eye with a blunt corkscrew?

Newspaper back in jacket pocket, I return to the ascent. Just as I reach the point where I will have to leave the path, a dog charges at me, barking furiously. It is small, mostly fur and pin-like teeth set in the face of a vampire bat. From the fuss it is making you might suppose I'd murdered its entire family. Or that my withered limbs offered a lifetime's supply of doggie treats.

This happens every other week. The small ones are always the worst. I move so slowly, you wouldn't think I could arouse the buried hunting instinct of the modern lapdog. And yet, I do. Their owners tell me they would never bite, and only want to play. I tell them it is a curious form of play. (Though, come to think of it, the pastimes of my youth included biting, once in a while, and excited yelping.) Sometimes I ignore them, sometimes I beat them off with my stick, which is guaranteed to provoke self-righteous fury in the owners – who, of course, have no right to bring their dogs here in the first place. Today – yesterday – I bend down, as if to pat the disgusting little rodent. It backs off, growling – a surprisingly deep-throated, guttural sound for something so puny – but I am too quick. I grab it by the scruff of the neck, slipping a permanently curled finger through the collar, and lift it to my chest. It struggles, but I press hard, taking care to keep the teeth on the outside.

I look around for the owner. ~He won't hurt you, says a man from behind me. He only wants to play. *Of course he does.* I turn slowly, carefully. The man is young and fit. He may lift weights. I would not have been surprised to see him with a bull terrier. I assume that this – this what? Chihuahua? – belongs to his mother, or perhaps his girlfriend. But what do I know? ~It's the stick, he says. I look down at my walking stick as if realizing for the first time that it is there. ~He thinks you want to play. ~Perhaps, I say. What is his name? ~Rocket. ~Well, Rocket, I say, stroking the tiny bat-like head but taking care not to loosen my hold on the collar, unlike your owner I don't claim to read the minds of dogs, even supposing you possess such a thing. ~He's very clever, says the young man. He can do tricks. ~You may be right. Little Rocket here may be a doggie Einstein for all I know, even if he's not bright enough to know the difference between an old man and a rabbit. No matter. He may, as you say, just want to play. But here's a thing: I don't care. I don't want to play with him. ~He won't do it again. It's just your stick. ~I'm not going to stop using a stick. I'm going to carry on walking. And if little Rocket here comes snapping round my ankles, do you know what I'm going to do? ~He's only playing. ~I'm going to pick him up like this - I hold the dog out by the collar; he yelps and waves his little paws uselessly - I'm going to cuddle him like this - I pull him back against my chest, tightening my grip on the collar as I do so - I'll pat him on the head and stroke his little nose, like this, and let him lick my fingers, and then, ever so gently, I'll break his fucking neck.

I drop Rocket at my feet, never taking my eyes off his owner. He steps forward and scoops up the dog, muttering: Mad old cunt.

I've been called worse.

I say, Are we clear? He steps back again, clutching the dog. ~You touch him, I'll fucking do you. Mad old cunt.

But he's talking to himself, not me.

What do I remember of that night? That Mayfair nightclub? And how much of what I remember is real, how much a montage of all the 60s retrospectives we've all seen ever since? There were dolly birds - I kid you not: those were the very words Councillor Simpson, Chairman of the Housing Committee, used - birds, girls, young women, with hair like space helmets, made up like Barbarella. One or two were wearing actual catsuits. Others had skirts like curtain pelmets – pleated and no longer than a hand's span. And the men? In those days, I liked to say the men fell into three categories: the young and groovy (another word Cllr Simpson used that night, possibly for the first time, judging from the way it stuck to his pendulous lower lip); the old and definitely square, most of whom were unaware of – or unconcerned by – the straightness of their edges; and finally, the sads: the squares, of whatever age, who wanted to be groovy. In this last camp I distinctly recall a pink-faced Etonian in a primrose yellow suit with a lime green polka dot cravat and white tasselled loafers. Which must be a real memory. There is surely nothing in my psyche capable of inventing *that*? There were one or two groovy old fuckers, too, and it was these who interested me the most.

Peter, of course. Peter was a groovy old fucker in his own quiet, understated way. Also, perhaps predictably, the older of the two Danish architects – although not their fellow countryman, a developer who owned the rights to their designs, and whose drunken humour did nothing to disguise his essential sadness. More improbably, Cllr Easton, Leader of the Council, and JJ's ultimate boss. Who would have thought it? At the party, the previous summer, he had been in work attire – a three-piece suit of no particular grace or style – and had avoided the dance floor. Tonight, without any flamboyance, there was something decidedly delicious about him.

Brian? Brian was there. But whatever qualities Brian possessed, grooviness was not amongst them.

And me? I was thirty-five. Today, that sounds impossibly young. But I was a man in my prime. In our party of ten, all male, apart from the junior Danish architect-cum-bag-carrier, I was much the youngest. And yet, in those days, in that first real flourishing of the cult of youth, we were all old. The difference between my thirty-five and Cllr Simpson's sixty-four was immaterial. Never trust anyone over thirty, the hippies would soon say. And they were probably right.

Who do you trust, Diana? Not me, certainly. Why on earth would you? Do you even know anybody under thirty? These days the young rail against the hippies for growing up, buying and selling houses for Monopoly money prices, stealing their pensions and trashing their planet. Peace? Love? They spit on it. I dare say Dad – your granddad, Diana – would have spat on it, too.

So I was already thirty-five on that cold January night in 1967, no longer young, but not yet old, not really. I was dressed down for a night out. There might be champagne, there might be music and laughter and gaiety to be found, but this was work and I was dressed *not* to stand out, dressed, in fact, in one of JJ's suits, that I had offered to have subtly altered around the waistband and the jacket pleats, reflecting his new, more substantial position in life, and which, calling on all the mutual obligations of our long association, I would have to beg Tomas even to touch. Life is too short, I always say – even my life, even now – for cheap brandy or inferior tailoring. But I wore it, your suit, and smiled as I was introduced to men I already knew, as Cllr Simpson told me to relax, I wasn't in the office now, as the dolly birds brought champagne to our table and the camera in the hands of one of the hangers-on flashed, momentarily blinding us and bleaching the scene with antiseptic light.

I smiled.

It had taken six months to bring these people here, together. Six months since your party, JJ. Six months of subtle nudges and none-too-subtle arm-twisting – your arms, mostly, even though we finally concluded, Brian and Peter and I, that it might be better that you not be there. Six months of encouragement and reassurance, of deciding in advance what would be decided there, that night. (Nothing would be decided there, that night. Decisions would be taken in committee, by committee members, contracts would be signed: by you, JJ, by you. I would be there, watching, in your office when you signed it with one of the fountain pens Mum gave us when we left London for the countryside. *My pen, not yours: they were identical, but mine has a scratch you made grabbing it off me, once. It shouldn't have been there, among your things.* What had she imagined we would write, out there amidst the pigs and the peasants? Letters home?)

Six months of patient work. Work not captured in the job description of a Quantity Surveyor, although the measurements involved – of each man's precise degree of ambition and greed and fear – were finely calibrated. More finely, as things turned out, than the tolerance margins in the system we were buying. Six months, starting with the party itself, and the morning after. Or rather, the week after, listening to you rant on about how Cllr Simpson had pitched up in your office on the Monday morning, more red-faced and bushy side-burned than ever, demanding to know if it was true that you could buy a Danish system high-rise for half a million quid? You'd said you would look into it. He wanted to know if it was true that you could put them up in weeks, and why you hadn't done it already. You pointed out that no one had, yet. You reminded him you'd only been in the job a matter of days, and he reminded you that you'd only got the bloody job in the first place because you weren't your predecessor, because you *would* get things done.

That's what you'd said in your interview, wasn't it? More or less?

You said it wasn't that simple, and he said, wasn't it? He said he was a simple man, who liked simple things, and it looked pretty bloody simple to him. You said you'd have to knock down the old houses first, and he said of course, he might be simple, he wasn't bloody stupid. Knocking those houses down was just the sort of thing you'd been appointed to get done. You accepted that, most likely with a nod, an instinctive placatory gesture of obeisance, but still said it wasn't simple, it would take time. There were people in those houses. That's the problem, Cllr Simpson said. They shouldn't be there.

Then you came and told me to stop fucking interfering in your job, in your whole council. I said, Me? What did I do? ~What *did* you do? ~Really? I said. I chatted to Tony. I danced with Frances. ~You introduced your smooth Hungarian friend to Cllr Simpson. Polish, I didn't say. I said: They introduced themselves. ~I'm telling you, Charlie. I'm warning you. If I want to buy a bunch of concrete slabs, I'll buy a bloody bunch of concrete slabs. I don't need your help. ~So you are interested? At which point Bee intervened, as I'd known, or expected, or hoped she would, with a glass of wine for each of us and a question about the film, or play or exhibition, or whatever it was she'd just dragged us to see, and you retreated into the silent grumpiness with which I dare say you'd endured whatever the show had been.

So I smiled.

Six months. And in a year from then, six months on, from that night in January when no decisions would be taken, and nothing would be done, just nine or ten men enjoying champagne and whisky and music and each others' company in a Mayfair nightclub that no longer exists, in a year from then, give or take a month or two, the Rochester Estate – four towers surrounded by low-rise maisonettes, homes for seven hundred and fifty families – the Rochester Estate would open its doors to the first lucky and unlucky tenants, including you, JJ (and Bee, of course), whose place in the ballot turned into a flat on the sixteenth floor of Rochester House itself.

It could have been worse.

Rochester: I like to think it was my private joke, adding a little fun to local government business. It's true I was the one who suggested the names to Cllr Simpson: Rochester, Dryden, Marvell, Congreve. ~Poets, I said. Dramatists. A touch of class. Nothing could be too good for working people, wasn't that what Bevan said? But really, it was Bee I had to thank. Via St Pancras. It was during that riot outside the Town Hall, after I told you I was moving to Wilmots and she told me I couldn't serve both God and Mammon. ~John Wilmot? she asked. ~Brian. The company's called Wilmots. Without an apostrophe. Don't ask me why. Perhaps there's more than one of them. ~John Wilmot, Bee said, was the second Earl of Rochester. ~And who was he? ~A poet. You'd like him.

I doubted it. I didn't always follow up Bee's attempts to broaden my cultural horizons, but finding myself at a loose end one day in a public library in Crewe, I searched the poetry section for both 'R' and 'W'. Finding nothing, I enquired of the stern librarian. From behind lorgnettes she explained that the library did indeed possess some works of Rochester, but did not display them on the public shelves. If I wanted to consult them, she said, looking me up and down in a way that suggested she knew exactly why I might, then I would have to apply, in writing. It might take two weeks, she said, for approval to be granted. I would not be in Crewe in two weeks' time – would not be in Crewe ever again, if I had my way – so I thanked her politely. She pressed her lips together, unsurprised. Back in London, I visited the bookshops of the Charing Cross Road.

Bee was right. I did like Rochester, although 'like' is too feeble a word to describe the sensation I experienced. Licentious, witty, cynical, cheerfully omnisexual. Determined to grab life in both fists and wring every drop of pleasure from it. A man who could write a poem about cottaging in St James Park, another on premature ejaculation – and wind up wishing "ravenous chancres" on his own cock. A man who rhymed "done't" and "cunt". *I hate the thing is called enjoyment*, I read, and never before had a voice boomed across the centuries to speak directly to my heart. I'd never thought I *had* a heart, in the sense that poets meant. Enjoyment – by which he meant orgasm – was so much less exciting than desire, consummation so much less fun than the pursuit of *all that's life and fire*. When I'd said *fun*, what I'd had in mind, I realized, was Rochester. Something like Rochester. At the time I didn't stop to wonder quite why Bee might be such a fan.

When Cllr Simpson agreed to the names and I explained the subtle flattery of the Wilmot connection to Brian, he was delighted, although he'd never heard of his namesake. ~What did he write? ~Oh, I said, a satire against mankind, among other things. ~Sounds good. (Satire had been very fashionable a couple of years earlier.) ~It will make for a good topping-out ceremony, I said.

Rochester was the man. Dryden, Marvell, Congreve: they were there to make up the numbers.

So, yes. I smiled.

I smiled as Cllr Simpson barged his way out of our booth, not waiting for me to stand up to clear his way; smiled as he returned from the toilets twenty minutes later, his face glazed and unusually pale. I smiled as Cllr Easton laid his hand on my shoulder, and then my knee, to emphasize some insignificant point. I smiled as the Danish developer signalled to one

70

of his hangers-on, who drew a heavy brown envelope from the briefcase he had been nursing all evening and placed it on the table, just fractionally nearer to the council side than to theirs (although, obviously, we were all on the same side here!)

A brown envelope, Diana. Yes, I know. An actual brown envelope. But what can I do? That's the way it was.

I smiled as Cllr Simpson froze while simultaneously sweating heavily, and Cllr Easton leaned back, away from the table, putting as much distance between himself and the envelope as the upright banquette seating of the booth allowed. I smiled as Peter nodded almost imperceptibly and as I reached out, picked up the envelope and weighed it on the palm of my hand, as the camera flashed and Brian called a waitress to order more champagne.

Don't judge me too harshly, Diana. I did nothing wrong. Not then, at least. Or not what you may think. Still, I might not mention this tomorrow.

I never suggested it, never advised it.

I told him he didn't have to take the flat. That day, the day he signed the contract with the pen our mother gave me, I told him. We had left his office at the town hall together, and he told me that he would take a flat in one of the new towers, just like the Danish developer said he should. ~He never said that. ~He said I could. ~Of course you could, I said. It doesn't mean you have to.

What actually happened was that the Dane, in answer to JJ's repeated questions, said that the system was so safe, yes, even at twenty-two storeys, he would live in it himself. JJ asked him if he did, in fact, do so. The developer shook his head and explained, sadly, that there were as yet no such towers in Denmark. By then, of course, it was all too late. The decision that had not been made in January had been made.

He said he had to live there. If he was going to build it, he had to live there. *All men would be cowards if they durst.* That's Rochester. Earl of. Less pornographic than most of his stuff. The stuff I remember, anyway. He meant we only strive to do the right thing out of fear of being caught. JJ already had a flat, I pointed out. A council flat. No one could accuse him of hypocrisy. Or cowardice.

Now – then – I stood at the window in the living room, watching the sun turn the river into gold. 'Waterloo Sunset' was everywhere at the time, but maybe not in your world, JJ? I said, You might lose this. It was the wrong tack, of course. You'd think, wouldn't you, after all those years, I'd have known my twin brother better? ~We'll take our chances in the ballot. I turned to Bee, but she was just as keen. ~We'll be in at the ground floor, she said. ~Dear God, I hope not. ~Not the flat – the community. We can help seven hundred and fifty families make their new homes. ~You could do that here. ~We could, but . . .

But they hadn't. She hadn't. JJ had been in the town hall all day and half the night, in his office, in committees, moving things on, getting things done, making things better. It didn't really matter where he lived. If he came across his neighbours anywhere it was in a report and they were in trouble of some sort – rent arrears, noise disputes, abusive behaviour. Or they were in the tenants' association – its chairman, perhaps – the sort who came to committee meetings to complain about repairs, or noise, or abusive behaviour, and he would nod to them, if they passed in the walkways, say good morning or good evening, but no more. It would not be appropriate to socialize, given his position. Still, he was making things better. That's what he did.

Bee had tried. She had more time, after school, after

clearing up and preparing the next day's lessons, and more desire, to be honest. Their neighbours were not just the subjects of reports: some were parents of the children she taught. She had seen them around the school gate, across the child-sized desks at parent-teacher evenings, explained to them just how well their son or daughter was progressing, or not, and asked if there were perhaps anything, outside of school, at home perhaps, that might, perhaps . . . ? She knew them. But when she'd joined the tenants' association – wife of the Deputy Director, and then Director; teacher of local children – she found herself an object of curiosity, regarded by the other tenants with a mixture of interest and suspicion. They might gain something, after all, from her position; but their wariness was genuine, and understandable. I dare say they heard her mother's vowels – "Lady" Antonia's vowels – as I no longer did.

Can you blame them?

She didn't know them, either. She knew about them.

Do you remember when I moved in here, Diana? To the Centre? You were under my feet, even then. The woman next door, Mrs. Vega, she asked you if we wanted a cup of sugar. We didn't – I never use the stuff – but you took it, didn't you? Because, despite everything, you were properly brought up. God knows how Angela managed it, but there you go. She raised Frances, too. Anyway, the point is, I didn't speak to her again – Mrs. Vega – for a month or so. Not till she knocked on the door, one night, to ask if I wouldn't mind not playing my records quite so loudly, or quite so late, and I said, no, of course. No, I didn't mind, I mean. We had a cup of tea and she told me about her late husband, who was Portuguese, she said. By which she meant Angolan, like herself, but white. She told me about the woman who'd lived here before me, briefly, and from whom I'd bought the flat. I told her about my parents and how we'd lived here – near here, just around the corner – a long time ago, before the war, and how we'd come here, as children, JJ and I, when it wasn't flats, when it was the Pioneer Centre. I told her about the Peckham Experiment, and she said yes, she'd heard all about that. She finished her tea and left and we didn't meet again for three or four months, although I could hear her sometimes, moving around in her flat, and I dare say she could hear me, although I kept the music down, and bought some headphones, and used them when it was late.

And that's how it should be, Diana. Mrs. Vega and I are friends. We don't see each other often, not deliberately, just on the doorstep, or in Tesco's sometimes, or the corner shop. We don't arrange to meet. But we talk, when we do meet. We are civil. It is pleasant. She has a set of my keys, and I have a set of hers, in case either of us locks ourself out, or, you know . . . We don't have to join a club. That's what I'm saying. To associate. We don't tell each other what to read, or eat, or think. I don't have to make her life better.

We are friends, I think. I'll go to her funeral. Or she'll go to mine.

This brandy glass is empty.

Bee wanted to start again, to try again. Though why she thought it would be any different I honestly don't know. She wasn't wrong though, was she? In the end? It did work out differently, even if all the things that happened would have to happen first. After that, she wound up chair of the tenants' association herself. She had no shortage of friends, although JJ was not among them. Not then.

And me?

I've never not loved Bee.

Why didn't I want them to move to the Rochester Estate?

I never said I didn't want them to. I just said they didn't have to. There's a difference.

Is there? Really?

I had no reason to warn them off. Oh, I know you think I did, Diana, but I didn't. Really – *don't say really* – the world isn't like that. It isn't full of evil masterminds and criminals and corrupt politicians who know exactly what they're doing. It's full of people who mostly haven't got a fucking clue what's going on. Nobody knows anything. Hindsight is deceptive. Looking back, it's easy: May, Cameron, Brown, Blair. But when you're there? Looking forward? Who can say who'll be next? Cameron, May, Corbyn?

Okay, that isn't going to happen. Tomorrow. When we return to the booths in the morning, however much the polls have narrowed, we're not about to expiate our collective sins. Her majority will be bigger than ever, and we'll get the Brexit we voted for. Or something like it. It'll get her in the end, though. If not Brexit, something. It was Enoch Powell who said all political lives end in failure, but we forget his caveat: unless they're cut off in midstream at a happy juncture. Happy? Happy before life is cut off, or because it is? Powell would have wondered, too. A man whose mother taught him Ancient Greek at five, who learned umpteen other languages and became a professor at 25, such a man used words with care. He would have wanted out of Europe, too. He never wanted in. Sometimes you can't choose who might agree with you.

In 1968 I was just the QS. I was in the room when the deal was done, in the office when the contract was signed. I'm sure JJ did his job. Yes, the blocks were cheap, but that didn't mean anyone was cutting corners. We were reinventing building. Once upon a time you built a frame, then filled it in. Now the walls and floors and ceilings – concrete panels the size of swimming pools – *were* the frame. There were no girders. No steel. You stacked the panels up, one on top of the other, boxes on boxes, higher and higher, and it was sheer weight that kept them in their place. Gravity, the engineer's eternal nemesis, was our friend. It had worked in Denmark. There was no reason it couldn't work here. True, the Danes had gone no higher than five or six storeys. They worked to a tolerance of no more than 1/25th of an inch in measurements of several yards. It wouldn't be like that on the eighteenth floor on a wet Friday afternoon with no scaffolding or safety net. The principle was the same though, wasn't it? So what if the wind's a bit stronger two hundred feet up? The contract never specified that the pair of H2 bolts attaching each panel to its neighbour should be properly tightened. It didn't *say* that the joints between them shouldn't be filled with cigarette butts, wax paper sandwich wrappers and old fag packets, rather than cement. *Some things don't need saying.* JJ wasn't responsible for that. He didn't ask for any of it. We're none of us perfect, Bee said. Except you, I said. Hindsight is common but imperfect, foresight vanishingly rare.

In April 1968, a few weeks after we finished building the Rochester Estate, Powell had other things on his mind. *In this country in fifteen or twenty years' time,* he told Conservatives in Birmingham, *the black man will have the whip hand over the white man.* Whip hand. He knew what he was doing. He always claimed he was quoting a constituent, "a middle-aged, quite ordinary working man". Even so. Even if the conversation really happened, he chose to report it. A man like Powell used words with care, even when they were other people's. He said he had no choice. He said those who shirked the duty of trying to avert *avoidable evils* would deserve the curses of those who came after. He had a choice.

He knew.

When Heath sacked him two days later, the London dockers – some London dockers – marched on Parliament with home made placards. *Don't Knock Enoch. 65,000 Dockers Back Powell.*

Did they? There were hundreds there, not thousands. Were they the same dockers who, a couple of weeks later, rushed to Ronan Point to rescue people trapped in the rubble, hauling away great slabs of broken concrete with their bare hands? Or, a fortnight after that, rushed a little less eagerly, no doubt, and with just a touch of *deja-vu*, to Rochester House? Or were those the dockers that the communist Jack Dash led in anti-Powell demonstrations? Who knows? Probably they were both.

Enoch was right has echoed down the decades, shorthand for hatred and bigotry and resentment and sheer frustration at the way the world has gone.

Powell for PM was painted on the walls, then.

Hindsight is never 20/20.

In 1968 most people in this country – seven in ten, or thereabouts – told pollsters they agreed with Enoch. So what about you, Diana? What would you have said? You were in your twenties, then, an adult already. You would have had no excuse. But I know what you'd have said. Because we were all properly horrified, us Jellicoes. Was this the country we'd grown up in? This more or less naked racism and bigotry?

Of course it fucking was.

The fascists might have lost at Cable Street, but they'd been there for the fight. They'd been in Notting Hill in the 50s and they were still there then, in 1968. They're still here now.

What would Robert and Catherine Peters have said? Or Elijah Johnson? Or Rabia Leel, or Beth or Gwyneth or David Williams have said? One of them – four or five of them, if the polls are to be believed – must have thought Enoch was right, that Enoch was the man they most admired in Britain, the best politician we had. And would have kept saying so well into the 1970s, at least. If they hadn't been dead.

Does that matter, Diana? Of course it doesn't fucking matter. No one deserves to see their kitchen wall pop out into the evening sunshine and topple eighteen floors, end over end onto the playground climbing frame below. No one deserves to watch their furniture or their children slide out after it as the floor collapses and they cling desperately on to the doorframe by their fingernails until the effort and the pain and the terror become just too much, or the ceiling and the flats above crash down and neither effort or pain or terror – or hope, despair, or prayer – make any fucking difference whatsoever in the face of sheer brutal gravity.

It matters – it makes a difference somewhere, surely? – that we knew about the problem before Ronan Point happened, even if no one had yet died. That by the time they did, it was old news?

We? Wilmots. Brian knew. I knew.

What happened was, it twisted, in the wind, and – of course – it moved. Tall buildings always move. The Post Office Tower was built to sway fifteen inches in a gale. Any more and the TV waves would miss their target – half of Britain would lose the Forsyte Saga. Fifteen inches might not sound a lot, but imagine it now, Diana. Imagine the floor under your feet shifting more than a foot while you try to stand still.

Steel is flexible. It bends, it sways. It's why engineers stopped using iron, which doesn't.

Concrete doesn't, either. Concrete doesn't bend. It can move, though, up to a point. Movement itself wasn't the problem. It was the twisting.

When a tower twists, it moves in different directions at the same time. Think about it. Think about the way a snake's skin ripples, or an armadillo's plates slide over one another. And that's all right – up to a point – if your building's made of small, flexible or articulated parts. But when each part is large, rigid and responsible for holding its neighbours in place? What happens then? What happens is they crack. Or, worse still, they pop out. Whole.

We knew. We knew because *it had happened*, while we were building Rochester House. By Christmas '67 it was two-thirds up. Boxing Day was unusually windy. When I arrived on site the next day, what should have been the living room wall of a fourteenth-floor flat lay shattered where it had fallen, crushing a couple of cement mixers and blocking off the ground floor access. No one was hurt, because no one had been there. At the time we put it down to the fact that we hadn't finished – there was no heavy concrete ceiling to keep the wall in place, and it had not yet been bolted in. Once each box was completed, we were sure – the Danes assured us – it would be secure. That's the way the system worked.

We carried on. What else could we do? We – Wilmots – reported the accident. But no one had been hurt. It was no big deal.

Afterwards, JJ claimed he never saw the accident report, and I for one believe him. I'm not convinced it ever reached his desk. Why would it? No one was hurt. By lunchtime we'd cleared away the shattered concrete. By close of play we were already on to the fifteenth floor.

He says if he'd known, he might have intervened. It's not

true, though, is it, JJ? What would you have done? What could you have done? By the time the report was written, and typed, and posted to the town hall – and delivered, and opened and directed to your office – we'd have been another three floors up. On time, and still on budget.

Hindsight.

Ronan Point was named after Harry Ronan, a local councillor. Poor bastard. Imagine what that must have been like, afterwards. Introducing himself. *Hi. I'm Mike Aberfan. Really? I'm Sergei Chernobyl.* Okay, different scale. But you get the point? You did, JJ. You did.

What happened at Ronan Point, a few months after our little on-site accident, was that a woman by the name of Ivy Lodge lit the gas under her kettle and blew the wall of her living room out into the early morning air. Scary, I imagine, but not the end of the world. She survived. But then the panels in the flats above, no longer supported by the missing wall, fell down onto the flats below, creating a progressive collapse, with panels popping out like slices of toast, and the entire south-eastern corner of the building folded in on itself, overlapping panels hanging like herringbone parquet, as if they'd been designed to fall that way, as if some dexterous close-magician had fanned his cards, inviting you to take your pick.

You'll have seen the photographs.

I love that phrase: progressive collapse. It's what we call it when a structural failure spreads through a building, like dominoes knocking down their neighbours.

Four people died that day – not Ivy or her husband; not the man two floors below who, improbably, surfed all the way to the ground on a slab of falling concrete – but the couple in the flat directly below Ivy's, and another from the top floor. A fifth died two weeks later, in hospital, the day before

Rochester House. It was only because it happened early – just before six in the morning – and these were living rooms, not bedrooms, that the numbers were so low, and *they rebuilt it*, Ronan Point. What else were they going to do? They braced the panels and took out the gas. We all did. But you didn't need a gas leak, an explosion. You just needed a strong wind. We'd already proved that, though we didn't know.

Until we did.

JJ spent the two weeks after Ronan Point around home, barely getting in to the office, but working his arse off all the same: talking to the tenants, talking to his neighbours, mostly for the first time, talking to Bee, telling them all it would be all right, that the system on the Rochester Estate wasn't the same, that they had electric heating, not gas, that we would learn the lessons anyway. That lessons would be learned. Errors corrected. That's how progress is made, he said. We try, we learn, we fail, we correct, we move on.

Structural redundancy. That's what Ronan Point and Rochester House taught us in the end. There has to be more than one way to hold a building up, just like a jet liner keeps flying when one engine fails. Nowadays, when a concrete panel collapses or a pillar gets blown out by a homemade bomb, or a fire guts your tower block, it won't fall down. You might be dead anyway, but it won't fall down. And that's progress.

But

On Saturday 1st June, 1968, that year of riots and revolutions, of assassinations and protest and war and peace and love and *Don't Knock Enoch*, exactly fifteen days after Ronan Point – when, by rights, it should never have been that windy, but it was – Rochester House collapsed. Robert and Catherine Peters, Elijah Johnson, Rabia Leel, and Beth and Gwyneth and David Williams died and everywhere we went Louis Armstrong's sunshine-and-gravel voice reminded us all what a wonderful fucking world it was. Their names are worth remembering – once again, for the record: Robert and Catherine Peters, Elijah Johnson, Rabia Leel, and Beth and Gwyneth and David Williams – even if their deaths were more than usually meaningless, there being no prize for coming second in the atrocity stakes; even if the lessons learned from Rochester House would be no different from those of Ronan Point, the policy U-turns no more permanent; and even if I won't, after all, recite them tomorrow – Diana's right, it wouldn't be *appropriate*, it's not their funeral; even so, they will be remembered for a while longer.

You never forgot, did you, JJ? You never let me forget.

This time next year, it'll be fifty years. Last year it was thirty since the whole estate came down. Is that why you went now? Why you died before me, even though you were younger? My little brother. I don't believe it.

For one thing, I'm not superstitious. More to the point, you refused to leave. You never left.

That's the point: you withdrew, but you never left.

That was your life.

It is dark, properly dark. Unusually, I must have fallen asleep. The desk against my cheek feels warm. The glass beside me is empty. It has left wet rings, blurring the ink on the page it sits on.

I raise my head, switch on the desk lamp. In the window I see an old man, grey hair shoved over to one side, drool hanging from his mouth. There is a reason for this.

It is almost midnight. I, who never sleep, must have slept for two or three hours. This seems unlikely. Where is Diana? Diana must have left, although I have no memory of her going.

Unless she is still here, lurking somewhere around the flat? This too seems unlikely.

I try to stand. My legs are more than usually unreliable, are still, it seems, asleep and unwilling to be roused. I slap at my thighs and jiggle my feet to restore the circulation. The doctor's got me taking so much Warfarin these days my blood must be like water. You wouldn't think it would have such trouble getting round. *I get around.*

I stand and slowly – there is no hurry – make my way into the kitchen. I turn on the radio for the midnight news. It is Election Day, but the moratorium on political coverage will not begin for a few hours yet. The polls are all over the place. Theresa May sounds more than ever like a Dalek. She's had a terrible campaign and deserves to lose, but I don't suppose she will. An eighth victim of the London Bridge attack has washed up in the Thames at Limehouse, like something out of an Edwardian melodrama. The poor man must have jumped off the bridge to avoid the van. Or perhaps he was flung over? A woman in Wanstead was attacked with a knife this morning, but the incident is not being treated as a terrorist incident. Terrifying, possibly, but only for her. The rest of us are not supposed to worry.

Personally, I don't.

I'm in the kitchen for a reason.

Tea! That's why I came in here. I shouldn't. I'll be dribbling in my pants all night, but what choice do I have? I won't sleep now. It's tea or brandy, and I'm not sure which is better. For my bladder, I mean.

I still have a eulogy to write. A panegyric. A *sua* – not a *mea* – *culpa*? Like Diana says, it's not about me.

My brother was a good man, surely? But his faults were my faults, his sins my sins: we were identical.

It's not just horror films that are full of twins: it's anthropology and psychological research. All those eighteenth-century thought experiments and twentieth-century studies into the development of separately-raised siblings. Nature versus nurture, innate nobility and original sin. But we were raised together, you and I. A Peckham experiment all of our own. When I look in the mirror, it's you I see.

I prop my stick, and then myself, against the counter where I can reach both the kettle and the sink. I let the tap run cold. Why? I'm only going to boil it. Is it a hangover from the days when we used lead in the plumbing? When water standing in the pipe became toxic? Maybe. I remember JJ once making tea for Dad. For a dare – because I didn't believe he would – he put a teaspoon of mustard powder in the cup along with the sugar. Dad took a sip, made a sour face and asked if he'd used fresh water in the kettle.

I told Bee this story once. JJ said it didn't happen; that it was me.

Which was it, JJ?

I up-end the pot and empty cold tea into the sink. Teabags like sodden turds block the filter. That must have been Diana. I tell her not to, I tell her those bags are made of plastic that will clog the oceans for centuries to come. As if I cared about centuries.

When they died, Bee said you should resign. Not *when* they died – you were far too busy then, consoling the bereaved, reassuring survivors, shifting families around like the tiles in one of those plastic puzzles where you have to rearrange the picture, and there's only one blank space. But afterwards. I said you should stay.

Peter wanted you to stay.

We had met – Peter, Brian and I – almost immediately,

the day after the day after the collapse. It was a brilliant June afternoon. The wind had died down over the weekend. There had been early summer showers in the morning, which helped settle the dust on the Rochester Estate, and left the rest of London bathed in warm, clean light, the outlines of the buildings and the buses unusually sharp, the colours for once living up to the promise of the psychedelic dream. For a Monday, Soho was incandescent. Mayfair looked as if it had combed its hair and pulled on its best party strides. But the narrow stairs of Peter's Georgian club were as dark and spongy underfoot as ever. In the small back room overlooking a brick courtyard full of catering bins and smoking kitchen staff, the sash window had been raised six inches, an insurrectionary response to the change in the weather. Outside, sunlight scoured the walls and bleached the curtain linings in the small back rooms of the building opposite. Inside, it turned a narrow, slanting column of dust motes into swirling fireflies that only thickened the surrounding gloom.

Peter seemed to have been ensconced there for some time when we arrived. He ordered a fresh pot of tea and gestured for Brian and I to sit. Brian remained on his feet, barely able to keep still, until Peter pointed again at a Chesterfield and it was clear that nothing would happen until Brian sat down. The leather upholstery creaked in the silence. ~It is a tragedy, of course, Peter said. ~Of course. What else could we say? ~Have you spoken to the Leader? Or Cllr Simpson? ~Not yet, Brian said. They'll have been run off their feet all weekend with the residents and the police and government inspectors. It hasn't been the time. Peter nodded. ~You should. ~Of course. Brian looked as if he'd rather have a quiet chat with Beelzebub.

The tea arrived, the waiter laboriously transferring

85

one-by-one the silver pot, milk jug, cups, saucers, teaspoons, sugar bowl, tongs, biscuits and a plate of tiny sandwiches from his tray to an occasional table beside Peter's chair. We waited in silence. When he left, Peter lifted the lid and stirred the pot, then turned to me. ~And your brother? ~We've spoken. ~How is he bearing up? ~Hard to say. He hasn't stopped working yet. Bee thinks he should resign.

Peter wasn't just being polite. He was genuinely interested in JJ, in how he was coping. But the mention of resignation brought an extra intensity to his attention. ~Has she said this to Jolyon? ~Not yet. ~But she will? ~I'm sure she will. After a pause, he said: That would not be helpful. ~It will cross his mind in any case. ~I meant his resignation, Charlie. His resignation would not be helpful. There is so much to be done. The inquiry is already underway at Ronan Point, and I'm told it will be swift. Hugh will report in the autumn.

I didn't ask. Hugh would be Hugh Griffiths, QC, the inquiry chairman. If Peter knew him, he didn't mention it, but there would have been no reason to. Then again: told by whom? ~Rochester House will be an addendum to that report, Peter said. One for engineers and civil servants to read. And you, of course, Charlie.

Brian said, And in the meantime? ~In the meantime, as I say, there is much to be done. Much rebuilding. ~Or demolition? ~I meant the wider landscape, Brian. Rebuilding of trust, of relationships. I don't think we should be discussing demolition. ~But who'd want to live there now? I had seen Brian under stress before, when deals looked like collapsing, when there were no cranes to be had for love or money, when plasterers or plumbers went on strike. I'd seen him shout and swear, but I had never seen him rattled. I had never heard Brain Wilmot suggest that people wouldn't want to live in flats that Wilmots built. ~According to JJ, I said, some of them don't even want to move out now. They're refusing to go. I didn't say that might be because they didn't trust the council not to dump them somewhere worse. ~It's a decision for the council, Peter said. But they have three other blocks. They may need improvements, to strengthen the structure, to reassure the residents. Rochester House itself can be rebuilt. As I say, much work. I don't think it will help anyone for your client to be thinking about demolition. Brian said he didn't even know if they were still our client. ~Brian, don't be obtuse. They need your help. ~They might not see it that way. They might just think they should sue us.

Peter was becoming impatient, although his voice remained pleasant, and calm. He said, You were in the nightclub when it was agreed. Did they look like men who were going to sue you? ~We hadn't killed anyone then. ~You're being ridiculous, Brian. You haven't killed anyone. I assume the building system and the specifications were all set out in the contract? I nodded. ~And who signed the contract? ~JJ, I said. ~And who will sign the contract for any rebuilding work? ~JJ.

So long as he didn't resign.

Bee said you should. I wondered if she were just afraid. It wouldn't be surprising. She'd lived in a block that had collapsed. You'd moved out of Rochester House by then, along with everybody else, but you hadn't gone far, just across the way to an empty flat in Congreve House. From your kitchen window, every morning, last thing at night, she'd have seen it, the herringbone scales of concrete panels lying flat against the side of Rochester House. You'd have seen it, too.

You said, Dad always believed in the inevitable collapse of capitalism.

Was that supposed to be a joke? You didn't laugh.

Bee said you should resign. It was a matter of principle, she said. Seven people are dead, JJ. Someone has to be accountable. The man I married had principles. I said: He still has. Bee threw up her hands and made a noise like an old steam engine in the films we used to watch. ~He has, I said. He wants people to live in better homes. He wants their children to grow up in clean, light space that's warm and dry. ~Tell that to the Williams children.

That's how it worked, then. The three of us, in Bee and JJ's flat, in restaurants, in pubs, discussing life the way we always had, discussing politics and housing and art and books and music and JJ's career. Bee and I discussing JJ as if he were not my brother, not her husband, but our child. As if we'd taken it upon ourselves to work out what was best for him. I don't know if he listened. He soaked it all up like a porous stone that lets the river flow over it, simply absorbing water and becoming heavier, harder to shift, but otherwise unchanged. Like old times, and yet. Bee had always teased JJ, cajoled him, but always, too, loved him and supported him. Looking back, it was not the same: if I'd looked I could have seen the crack, the first sign of a marriage twisting in the wind. Perhaps I did.

I told Bee and JJ that much the bravest thing was to stay put, stay in the line of fire, as it were. Resignation would be self-indulgent. To help the tenants, to support the inquiry, to put things right and to go on building more, building better housing for the people who needed it most. To accept responsibility. To bear the weight and not succumb to progressive collapse. Structural redundancy, I said, that's what we need. Not actual redundancy. When one part fails, another holds the building up. The truth was – *the truth was neither here nor there.*

What did JJ say? In truth, not much. But he didn't resign. In the end, he threw himself back into work, more committed than ever.

In the end? After a while, I should have said. In the end there'd be a different story.

The tea has steeped long enough. I pour a drop of milk into a mug and half fill it. Cups and saucers are all very well for vicars and such, but not much use when you need one hand for a stick and the other's liable to shake like a junkie alcoholic under Hungerford Bridge in winter.

The truth was, I wanted you to stay, and you stayed. Whether there was any connection between these two facts no longer matters. Tomorrow, whatever Diana thinks, I will talk about your staying put. There's nothing wrong with staying put. It was the bravest thing you ever did, until you walked away.

It is quiet now, by London standards. That is, the music from a passing car, or the wail of sirens, is more distinct, standing out in greater relief, than it would during the day. Where I live there are three hospitals, two cop shops and a fire station all within walking distance. Not the sort of distance I used to walk, just because I could. To Camberwell, to Lewisham, to London Bridge. Because, even when I owned a car, I didn't always want to drive. In South Kensington, in Chelsea, I drove, with the top down whenever the rain allowed, precisely because it was not necessary. In southeast London I preferred to stroll, a boulevardier of the Old Kent Road, observer of the vast and dusty retail sheds, the chicken shops and Peruvian restaurants, the supermarkets and convenience stores offering international money transfers, the optimistic night clubs and the drive-in McDonalds, the few remaining Victorian buildings: a church; a fire station that was converted years ago into a cast-iron fireplace emporium, re-selling the cannibalized remains of its former neighbours; a handful of pubs. The Dun Cow: now a doctor's surgery. The Thomas à Becket: now a restaurant that, according to the gaudy poster in the casement window, offers cocktails in a goldfish bowl with long enough straws for four young women in tight clothes to share. A six-storey Peabody block called the Waleran Flats, like some unattractive corner of Missouri. So much to savour. And *still* you wonder why, even now, when I have to do it on a scooter, I spend my afternoons trailing idly up and down from the Aldi to the Elephant?

Half a mile from here, the Old Kent totters into New Cross Road. On Sunday night a woman was shot in the head just there, and miraculously survived. Miraculously? How easily we use these words, or allow these words to use us. I don't know the details of the wound or whether the victim considers herself fortunate. I only know I don't believe in miracles. But the shooting happened in the car park of a 1930s light industrial unit now converted into an evangelical church, so it's possible she does.

I'm no more afraid of random shootings than I am of terrorist attacks, or fires, or building collapse. These things happen, of course, but there's no reason to suppose that they will happen to me.

JJ asked what Dad would have done. ~Dad? Why? ~He was a man of principle, wasn't he? And that – a few days after my conversation with Peter and Brian, while the rubble was still being carted away from Rochester House – was when I knew Bee had spoken to him. That I would have to up my game.

I said, If you call Party infallibility a principle. We were standing side-by-side at his living room window in Congreve House, gazing out at the evidence.

~Don't you?

I didn't ask what he meant, because I knew. Ever since the day in Moss Bros when I said I'd joined the Party, we'd played a game in which, from time to time, I would pretend to make up things about my communism and he would pretend to believe me. I don't think he ever really knew whether I paid my subs or not. Just then, though, it was difficult to keep up with the rules of the game. It was 1968, Dougie, June: the riots in Paris had only just ended; Spring in Prague had another couple of months to run before the Soviet tanks would roll across the border and Dubcek and the rest of them be hauled off to Moscow. Who could know how Dad would have dealt with it all? He'd had the grace to be bombed by Nazis while they were still his party allies. If socialism had a human face, it probably wasn't that of your grandfather.

I said, Democratic centralism isn't always easy, comrade. ~Or democratic? ~Well, that depends. ~On what I mean by democracy? Really, Charlie? ~Don't say really. ~What? ~That's what Mum always said: don't say really. It makes you sound common. ~We *were* common.

We were wandering from the topic, but now I saw an opportunity. Sometimes the principled gesture can just be bourgeois affectation, I said. JJ laughed, briefly and without much humour. ~You think so? ~I'm so pure, I said, hamming it up, clasping my hands over my heart. I'm so special. My purity is *so* much more important than my contribution. ~What is your contribution, Charlie? ~I build houses. ~That fall down. We both thought about that for a moment. Then I said, And need rebuilding.

As it happens, the Party – the British party, my party

- opposed the Soviet invasion of Czechoslovakia. The leadership warned against it, and condemned it when it happened. The party line was clear, Dougie. There were plenty of members who disagreed, who thought Dubcek was the dupe of Western imperialism, or worse. Did they resign? Did they bollocks. When the leadership supported the action in Hungary in '56, thousands had left. Now, most of those who would have supported the leadership's judgment then, but opposed it now, did not. It was their party, too, Dougie. Our party. Resignation would only play into the hands of the anti-Soviet elements. Resignation could only preserve the ideological purity of those who did not at heart know that, whatever its faults, there was no correct position outside the party.

Your Uncle JJ, however, said nothing. It was not his party.

1968 ground on and on – the shattering events you might think you know about, Dougie, were all pretty much played out by the summer. The Tet Offensive? January. Grosvenor Square? March. Martin Luther King shot dead in Memphis? April, along with the "Rivers of Blood" and flogging London Bridge to the Americans. The Kray Twins getting arrested for shooting Jack "the Hat" McVitie? May. Bobby Kennedy? June. Czechoslovakia? As we know, August. The Isle of Wight Festival? August. The rest of the year was just a grating, dragged out diminuendo, anaesthetized repetition, tit-for-tat nuclear tests, Northern Ireland's descent towards chaos, John Lennon singing 'Happiness is a Warm Gun' and The Rolling Stones bleating about street fighting as if they'd just invented it. And what was actually playing all over the radio, all over everywhere to round off the year? *Lily the bastard Pink*, that's what. Four weeks at number one. If the human race needed salvation, it wasn't coming from Roger fucking McGough and

Paul McCartney's little brother. A perfect end to a grim year during which JJ said less and less about little or nothing. He went to the town hall, worked ten or twelve or fourteen hours and returned to the flat where he would stand at the window gazing out at the now empty Rochester House, watching the scaffolding ray-ay-ace slowly up to engulf it all.

He knuckled down. He got on with the job. He made the world better.

I had won. Bee had lost. Perhaps. In any case, he hadn't resigned.

Perhaps I should substitute The Scaffold for whatever tasteful Bach Diana has arranged for tomorrow? God, no. But would a crematorium these days have Bluetooth? With Dougie's phone – and Dougie's help – the possibilities would be endless. 'Ring of Fire': Johnny Cash. Or just: 'Fire'. '68 again. The Crazy World of Arthur Brown.

JJ never cared much about music. I mean, he didn't *dis*like it. You can't dislike music in the abstract, surely? That would be like saying you don't like food. You can only object to specific instances or classes of either: seafood, perhaps, or acid jazz. But he didn't much like it either. He had no strong opinions. I find that difficult to understand.

How can you live to be eighty-five and not hate anything but poverty and shoddy housing?

At the end, his end, in the hospital, they played a lot of *golden oldies*, which appeared to be a very broad church indeed, encompassing both Vera Lynn and Phil Collins. Sometimes they'd play *calm classical*, worried no doubt that Shostakovich might cause carnage in the geriatric ward. I remembered reading about the way the Underground uses piped music to install peace or, at busy times, to speed the flow of passengers with marching tunes. Would the management of an over-crowded hospital be tempted to free up beds with a little heavy metal? Perhaps things never got tight enough while JJ was there – it was spring, after all, the worst of the winter pressures long past – and it seemed to be all Pachelbel's Canon and Paul Simon. Which nearly finished me off, but washed through JJ like a saline drip while he – at most – muttered against the dying of the light.

Do I have to do a deathbed scene? Tomorrow, I mean. Some dying words? Did he go the way he'd always wanted to? I doubt he wanted to; or not to, for that matter. Did nothing in his life become him like the leaving it? It may have done.

You or I, Dougie – if we chose to die at all – might elect to go at a hundred and nine, crashing a micro-light into a mountainside in a freak, amphetamine-fuelled accident, or blocking the path of a mounted, baton-wielding police charge into the heart of an anti-fascist protest. We might. It is possible.

JJ had 'flu. Despite, I have no doubt, having had the jab. Indifferent as he may have been to his own survival, he'd have died obedient as ever to the nostrums of the welfare state. And he'd voted, I know that, he'd sent his postal ballot in good time for tomorrow. Being dead wasn't going to get in his way.

Were his loved ones gathered all around him? Well, I was there. And Diana. Angela, of course, had long been dead herself, Tony too, as far as I know. Not that it matters. Frances was in Barnes – not exactly the other side of the world, but far enough to reduce the frequency of visits to her uncles. I've never understood why a niece of mine would live somewhere like Barnes. I imagine Philip the detective had something to do with it; they moved when he retired at what I always took to be a suspiciously early age, but which Frances assured me was absolutely normal for the Flying Squad. She was still working at Broadcasting House, commuting in and out. I asked JJ when he'd last seen her, and was pleased to hear that it had been Christmas. She'd come to visit me in February, and again in early May.

And Dougie? Where was Dougie? Or Bee, for that matter? They'll all be there tomorrow. The family. Not Bee.

He sat up in bed, grey-faced like a pope. Diana handed him a glass of water and offered to help plump his pillows. He said: I don't need any help.

And those, I swear - whatever Diana says tomorrow - those were his final words.

This isn't helping. The kettle boils, I warm the pot and empty it again, spoon in the tea and set the kettle to boil again. Then, deciding on brandy after all, I pour a glass and carry it without much spillage to my desk, and return for the bottle. I tap the trackpad on my laptop and, when it returns to life, I type: *My brother Jolyon was nothing if not dogged.*

You'll give me that at least, Diana?

He carried on, more dedicated than ever, and Peter Sack, for one, was pleased enough; Bee less so, it was obvious - she made it obvious, she told JJ he had no spine, which seemed to me the opposite of the case. She said if we did not accept responsibility for our mistakes, what hope was there? And he said, if mistakes were made

if I made mistakes

if he'd made mistakes, his responsibility was to put them right.

I made mistakes.

At this point she may have thrown something, an ashtray or a coffee cup, she may have pointed to the window, beyond the window, to where JJ's men were slowly, painfully, detaching one by one the dangling concrete panels before allowing them to fall a hundred feet to the ground, each landing with a bowel-churning thud that shook the earth like heavy artillery, or she may have simply sighed and shaken her head. In fact she may have done all three, because this was a scene, an argument that was repeated many times.

It hurt him, I could see. To disagree with Bee. He loved work; he loved Bee. Oh, Diana, sweet Dougie – when we spinsters describe dedicated men as married to their jobs, we don't mean it as a compliment. But how are we supposed to understand the way they work? When JJ's job let him down, he didn't see it that way. He thought he was the one caught cheating.

Peter was right. Rochester House would not be demolished, and neither would Congreve, or Dryden or Marvell, and Bee would be outraged, again, and say you have to knock them down ~And lose five hundred flats? ~They're deathtraps. We're all living under a volcano, JJ. Any day now someone's going to want to hang a picture up, they're going to bang a nail into a wall and the wall's going to fall out and we're *going to die.* ~You're being hysterical, JJ said. ~Am I? And I nodded, which probably wasn't helpful, in the circumstances. I said, Well, perhaps. It would take more than a hammer, though. ~Oh, great. ~What I mean is, we can make them safe. We can add brackets to hold the panels together better. We can re-build the missing corner from the bottom up, a stand-alone tower, and then tie it into the main building with steel bolts, like a missing tooth. I knew the spiel because I'd practised and practised and practised before pitching it to Cllrs Easton and Simpson, neither of whom, as far as I know, had contemplated resignation for one second, and –

~*We?* ~Wilmots.

Bee laughed, or barked, I wasn't sure which. ~Really?

– don't say really – Really? she said to JJ, that's just marvelous, that's just fucking marvelous, and –

it was, really, an elegant and relatively inexpensive engineering solution. A commercial triumph, in the circumstances, though it took some doing, some long nights and more persuasion, but in the end the councillors – if not JJ – recognized the benefits we laid out for them, Brian and I, with Peter's invaluable advice. They saw the wisdom of keeping us close, of allowing or requiring us to correct our own mistakes, if, indeed, mistakes had been made.

Bee saw the matter differently, at least at first. She started going to the tenants' association again, staring down those who told her she shouldn't be there, because – *because of who she was, of who her husband was.* She declared her interest loudly and frequently, and through sheer force of will she won them over – she was her mother's daughter, after all. She denounced the council, she denounced JJ, her husband, *Yes, my husband,* he'd put all their lives, our lives, at risk for money, not his money, the council's money: their money, our money, when you got down to it. They'd wanted to do things on the cheap with our money and our lives. She denounced Wilmots, she denounced me – her brother-in-law, *Yes, my brother-in-law, yes* – as profiteers, as jackals, scavenging and feasting on their neighbours' deaths. She had her class paint banners again, this time featuring coffins and ruined buildings and bleeding pound signs, which some of the parents thought was going too far and for which she was formally reprimanded by the head teacher, but *she would not stop.* She demanded that, if no one was to be held accountable for seven deaths, if there were to be no manslaughter charges, if the buildings – if these *deathtraps* – were not to be demolished, if they were going to keep living here, then the council's contractors, Wilmots, should be forced to do the repairs and the refurbishment and the safety works to the highest possible standards, the highest specification. She got hundreds of tenants to say the same thing, to demand, outside the town hall with their placards and their megaphones, that cost be no object, that nothing could be too good, too safe, for working people, that money had to be spent and – in this, at last, our interests coincided once again . . . and I saw the wisdom of Peter's ways.

We were happy to work to whatever standard we were paid for; for their part, the councillors could not afford *not* to employ us. They'd been there, after all, in the nightclub, in the photographs, even if it wasn't their hand on the envelope

it was yours

but the thing is, no one was supposed to die.

It took almost four years, in the end. Which, frankly, was a bit of a miracle in itself.

It would have made sense to do Rochester House first, given it was empty. It was the obvious place to start. We could have made it safe, made it better than ever, made it lovely and filled it with everyone from Congreve House, then sorted Congreve out, moved tenants from Marvell to Congreve, then Dryden to Marvell, the tenants from Rochester into Dryden and – bingo! – job done, complete. Everyone would have moved, but most of them just once, and – no. Bee said everyone, EVERYONE must end up living in the flat they'd started in.

Not everyone.

As usual, the argument began at home, in Bee and JJ's kitchen before it ever reached the town hall. I said, What difference does it make? ~These are people's *homes*, Charlie. ~Since April, I said. Two months. They'll be decanted out longer than they'll have been in them to begin with. ~Decanted? They're people, not wine. ~You know what I mean. They'll have a flat, it'll be exactly the same as the flat they left. ~Except it won't be their home. ~This makes no sense, it *will* be their home, that's exactly what it will be. I looked to JJ, who was not looking at either of us. I said, it's a system build, they're all the same: that's the point. ~People aren't, she said, *that's* the point. And I gave up. She was wrong, but she was on a mission and I wasn't going to change her mind. As usual, JJ said pretty much nothing. He would put things right; that was his job. She persuaded Cllr Simpson who persuaded Cllr Easton who persuaded or instructed JJ – who, it's fair to say, probably did not put up much of a fight, so . . . we wound up leaving Rochester House till last, doing the blocks in the wrong order, an order that made no sense, that was more complicated, and slower, that made people move more often and gummed up the waiting lists, while leaving, at any given time, the occupants of two blocks and all the surrounding low-rise to wake up every morning for the best part of four years to the sight of Rochester House, partially collapsed and covered in scaffolding: every morning, every evening, a reminder that perhaps not everything was for the best in the best of all possible worlds, an object lesson in human fallibility, in the limits of rational systems to protect us from all risk, in the frailty of human life, a brutalist memorial to those who'd died, which was no doubt very salutary and good for their immortal souls and all, but must, frankly, have been a bit of a bummer.

My glass is empty. And so, dear God, is the bottle. At the back of the cupboard there is another, one I haven't opened and never expected to, one that will be quite vile – which would be disappointing if I'd bought it myself, but is somehow worse because it was a gift, from Mrs. Vega. A few years ago, her daughter took her to Portugal for a month; while she was away, I watered her spider plants and even – once, as ordered – the cacti in her bathroom. I felt like one of those poor souls you hear being patronized on *Gardeners' Question Time* when you can't make it to the radio fast enough to turn it off, which these days can be quite a problem. (On bad days I have suffered entire episodes of *The Archers* in the time it takes to rise from my chair and cover the ground between my table and the kitchen, where my old radio sits on a shelf beside the fridge. Dougie recently bought me a digital radio with a remote control, which was kind, but is another thing to lose.) When she returned, rather than ring the doorbell – which would have required me to make my way down the entire spiral staircase just to open the door to talk to her, to receive her gift, and her thanks – she waited until she heard me fossicking about in the hallway with my mobility scooter, preparing for one of my forays to the shops or to cruise the pavements of Peckham or the Old Kent Road, which was thoughtful of her, too, I must say. There are good people in the world. She said, I know you like brandy, holding out a duty free carrier bag. How had she known? We had been acquainted for years, even then, but I am sure – fairly sure – that we had never shared a drink. Perhaps, on the rare occasions she had been inside my flat, she had been unusually observant? Or perhaps she rummaged through the communal bins, examining the jetsam of my life. It seems unlikely, to be honest, but she was not wrong, and it is not her fault that she knows less about brandy than she does about me. It's not that it is Portuguese, or even Spanish, the brandy, which would have been bad enough, I dare say. It is South African, and not really brandy at all, more a puny, sickly sweet concoction of brandy-coloured effluent, decorated with gold. By which I do not mean the bottle was decorated, but the contents. ~Turn it upside down, she said, smiling at me more innocently than anyone of her age by any rights should smile, and you'll see. The bottle in my hand was in the shape of a flattened dome. I turned it over, tentatively – not something I would have done to a half-decent Armagnac – and lo! flakes of gold slipped slowly back and forth, and forth and back, as they settled, like a caramel snow globe. ~Thank you, I said, and she smiled. What else could I say? I invited her in for a cup of tea, but she said no, she could not possibly, she knew I was on my way out. She had just wanted to catch me, and thank me. ~Well, thank you, I said, again. ~No, thank you, and the bottle has remained untouched ever since because, however implausible, it is not impossible that Mrs. Vega might after all check the contents of the bins, and I would not want to hurt her feelings. I suppose I could have shown it to Frances, or offered a glass as a joke to Dougie, but I found, to my surprise, I did not want to. It would have felt disloyal. But neither did I want to drink the filth myself, of course, so there it stayed, at the back of the cupboard, until now. When, for the first time I can remember – and, believe me, its not the sort of thing I'd forget – I have run out of booze – real booze, acceptable booze – because, let's not beat about the bush, in the last couple of weeks I've had more cause to drink than usual, more reason not to notice the dwindling supply and less opportunity to re-stock.

And why is that?

Well, there's your untimely death for starters, JJ. That and everything it brought crashing along in its wake, if you'll pardon the pun. Not least more and longer visits from Diana. Plus telephone calls from relatives and friends and colleagues I haven't spoken to in years, not all of whom seem to be aware of the time differences involved, or the sheer effort of remembering how they all fit into the story of your life, which has been exhausting, not to mention dealing with so many of them cheerfully claiming that you'd had "a good innings" – what on earth do they think that says about me? Plus, there's been the hysterical pace of the news, the exercise of will-power required to keep up with it all, the terrorist attacks, the General Election campaign, the arguments – again, would you believe, after all these years, these decades – about whether councils should build houses, about leaving the European Union, about whose misremembered dream of the 1950s – *mine or yours* – we should be condemned to re-inhabit. So you'll forgive me if my domestic arrangements have been less than perfect. At least I've managed to change my underwear and eat more than porridge. I suppose I could have asked Diana to pop up to the corner shop, but generally I try not to. It's the pursing of her lips, the unspoken reminder of Angela's fate that I can't stand. If I were going to drink myself to death, does she not think I'd have done so by now?

Four years, best part of. People say a lot of things about the 1960s. They say if you remember them you weren't there, they say they died at Altamont, they say they really happened in the 70s, but I know Rochester House collapsed on the 1st of June, 1968, I remember that, and we held the grand re-opening party on Saturday, 19th February, 1972, as planned. I'm not likely to forget that, either. It wasn't a great time for a party, but after all the disruption and sheer hard work, everybody wanted to celebrate.

Everybody?

Even you, JJ.

In November, Poulson had filed for bankruptcy. Which was when we all discovered the G in J.G.L. Poulson and

Associates stood for Garlick. ~I know we don't have much of a leg to stand on here, I said when JJ told me, but what *were* his parents thinking? Inside, however, I felt a lurch, as if the foundations were shifting. Brian told me not to worry. We did no business with Poulson, but that wasn't what I was afraid of. Peter told me not to worry, too. He said it quietly, as he said everything. It was impossible to know whether he meant it or not.

We were supposed to finish before Christmas, but of course we didn't. Of course we didn't. This wasn't some minor refurb we were doing – patch a few holes and a lick of paint – this was a forty-two month programme and you had to expect some give and take. It didn't help that once we slipped past Christmas, the miners went on strike and the power cuts started. The first week in February, with the paint not yet on the walls, let alone dry, it was definitely touch and go when the Government declared a state of emergency, Iceland kicked off the Cod War and Heath scraped us into the Common Market by making it a vote of confidence, I remember that. It was less than a month since Bloody Sunday, and – Christ, what a time to be alive, let alone to hold a party.

JJ wanted to postpone, but that was just nerves. Besides, Bee wouldn't let him. The tenants association was raring to go. There'd be stalls, games for the kids, a tombola. The baking had already started. In the evening there'd be barrels of beer and wine and sandwiches in the tenants hall and not one, not two, but three local bands were lined up to play. It would be a night to remember. ~What if it's not finished? ~It'll be finished, I said. Even if it isn't, we won't be far off. We can still celebrate. We were in the kitchen again, JJ and Bee's kitchen, inspecting what would be their new kitchen, on the eighteenth floor of Rochester House, in the flat where Beth and Gwyneth and David Williams had lived, where all of this had started. It was JJ's idea. I could see his point – if he was going to live on the estate at all, where better? Even Bee could see his point. But now – then – I wondered if he was getting cold feet. ~We can't have a party in a state of emergency, he said. ~It's not *our* emergency, Bee said. Which was not quite true – it had been all hands to the pump at King Street since the strike started – but this wasn't the moment to quibble about the need for solidarity. ~What if there's a power cut? There's bound to be a power cut. ~We've got lanterns, Bee said. ~They're a safety hazard. They'll get knocked over. ~We'll hang them on the walls, out of reach. ~But there'll be booze and dancing and God knows what. In the dark. We'll burn the place to the ground and everyone will die. We'll have killed them all. Not just some.

I let that pass. ~We're builders, I said. We've got generators.

He knew this. It wasn't the first time we'd had this conversation. In the end, though, we were both right. There was a power cut, and *it was fine*. At least, no one died.

We finished the work with three days to go, just as the CEGB announced the power cuts would be longer from now on – nine hours at a time – but we were prepared. The weather worked out, too – that clear cold bright air you sometimes get, even by the river, cold as a witch's tit, of course, but with just enough forgiveness to let you believe spring might come again, in anticipation of which we'd planted a skip-load of bulbs in all the open spaces we hadn't actually concreted over. The daffs hadn't quite made it, but there were crocuses and snowdrops.

In the afternoon there was fun and games, just as Bee had threatened. Cllr Simpson, in an execrable brown safari suit and desert boots – where *did* he think he was? – unveiled a discrete plaque in memory of the tragic events of the first of

June, as he coyly put it, and then a school choir sang 'I'd Like to Teach the World to Sing'. Which was top of the charts and you honestly wouldn't think anyone needed to hear any more often than we already had, but neither that nor Cllr Simpson could lower the mood. Angela was there, still alive, then, if rather yellow. Was she proud of her little brothers? She said she was. ~Look what you've done, she said, flinging her arms out as if to hug the entire estate. The pair of you. ~There'll be wine later, I said. She winked and tapped her handbag.

Frances came. With Philip. She hugged me when she said hello. ~How's TV? ~Hellish. ~Really? ~Not really. I love it, but it's hard, with Dougie. Someone at the Beeb had spotted her gumption and moved her into production shortly before she got pregnant and they tried to get rid of her again. ~You didn't bring him? ~I wanted to. Philip thinks it will go on too late, so we left him with the neighbours. Philip wants to stay for the drinking. ~I hope he thinks it's worth it. Wilmots bought the wine. ~Philip's a beer and whisky man. ~Of course he is. There was a bit of a silence between us after that before I said: How old is Dougie now? Frances laughed, relieved. ~He's five. What kind of an uncle are you? ~A great uncle, I said, which was technically true.

Bee was in her element. Even in a maxi dress of some floaty, brightly patterned fabric, an Afghan coat and an orange headband, she gave the impression of hosting a royal garden party. We clinked glasses of fruit juice – it was three o'clock in the afternoon at that point. ~Your mother would be proud, I said. She kissed me on the mouth – she may have been aiming for my cheek – and asked me to introduce her to George, who wasn't called George, not that day. Her sunglasses were small and round and pink and entirely for show.

Even JJ looked happier that afternoon than he had for four

years – happier, perhaps than at any time since Herefordshire – chatting to his neighbours, shaking Brian Wilmot by the hand, hovering at the councillor's elbow while he spoke to a reporter from the *South London Press*. But, even so, he couldn't help reminding me it would be dark by five. I told him not to worry, it would all be fine.

And it was fine – *no one died* – though I dare say he still worried.

When the inevitable power cut came, the generator kicked right in and – for good or ill (opinions were divided) – the night's first band barely missed a beat. Bee insisted on lighting a few of the lanterns, just for show – for atmosphere, she said – and even though one of them did get broken – by George, as it happens, the result of some ridiculous prank – it didn't start a fire. He simply pissed on the flame, he boasted to me later, and everything was safe. I didn't pass that part on to JJ. The second band was not a band, it was a crooner and his accompanist. ~Something for everyone, Bee said. ~So long as everyone loves Andy Williams. ~Be fair. He does some Perry Como, too. The third band, though, surprised me, surprised us all, I shouldn't wonder. There were five of them, five lads, it looked like, not one of them old enough for sex – not legally, even then, after the Act, not the sort of sex I had in mind – and yet they sounded as if they'd been playing together for years. They kicked off with – what? 'Lola'? It could have been, but wouldn't that be just too obvious? – with Juliette Greco, then took requests, right after that, and seemed to know everything. The Beatles and the Stones, of course, and 50s rock'n'roll, but also jazz standards and Dylan and T Rex and Nat King Cole and music hall favourites and Pink Floyd and even, at the insistence of a child of nine or ten who really shouldn't have been exposed to such a scene at all, made a decent fist of 'Ernie (The Fastest Milkman in the West)'. The spectacle of the singer – whose glossy black hair was cut into an immaculate page boy bob, who wore a white silk blouse (you really couldn't call it a shirt) under a slightly too-large double-breasted suit and looked for all the world like Louise Brooks at her most alluring – standing centre stage, motionless, while mouthing Benny Hill's puerile innuendo in a voice that hovered somewhere above a baritone but also soared without apparent effort to a flawless countertenor, was one I knew would stay with me forever.

They surely hadn't been alive long enough between them to have absorbed this much music? The singer announced they'd take a couple more and I couldn't resist. ~It's a party, I said. Do you know 'Saturday Night Fish Fry'? ~Louis Jordan? Sure. They did, too, and 'Jack, You're Dead', which I hadn't even had the heart to ask for. I watched him – *her?* – sing and smile and never break a sweat while working the crowd and, for a moment, I thought I was in love.

I was forty years old. Which, in 1970s years, meant about a thousand. ~What's your name? I asked, when they finally finished their set. She smiled and pointed towards the back of the makeshift stage where the skinny drummer with arms like a lumberjack's was dismantling his kit. Across the bass drum it said: *The Postboys.* Dear God, I thought. ~There's a poem, I said. Rochester. ~We know, he said. She said. We live here, in Rochester House. ~*Son of a whore*, I said, *God damn you, can you tell/A peerless peer the readiest way to Hell?* And after the barest of pauses – more, I thought, for effect than straining for memory – she replied: *The readiest way, my lord, 's by Rochester.* We thought it would make sense, she said – to be the Postboys. Just for one night.

I'd been working flat out for months, I'd barely noticed

Christmas – apart from bastard Ernie and his fucking milk cart – I deserved a prize, of course I deserved a prize. But I'd never expected to find a gift so perfect. Could this Postboy possibly be real?

I said: I meant *your* name. That smile again. ~Are you the housing guy? ~That's probably my brother. ~You look alike. ~As two peas. ~Then how do I know which one you are? he said. ~I smiled, full beam. You'll have to trust me. What *is* your name? ~George, she said. What's yours?

~He's Charlie, said Bee, crashing into the conversation and linking her arm through mine. She smiled broadly. We were all smiling, one way or another. ~I'm Bee, she said.

Later, when the band had cleared its gear from the make-shift stage and Bee was dousing all the lanterns, Cllr Easton turned up, demanding to know where the party was moving on to. He had a friend with him, or a colleague, a man I hadn't seen before. After a moment, JJ said: Our place.

There were no lights, of course – there was still no power – but Bee said they had candles. There were no lifts, but somehow we made it up eighteen flights, carrying as many unopened bottles as we could hold or fit into our pockets, the chemical smell of fresh paint clogging our lungs, our shoes no doubt leaving the first scuff marks on the pristine linoleum. The ward councillors, the Leader and the Leader's new friend, JJ, Bee and I, Brian, Frances, Philip and a couple of dozen neighbours and friends and hangers-on trudged upwards in the dark together, gaily at first, joking and remembering the Blitz – or pretending to – but not George, my George, who wasn't called George and had disappeared somewhere in the course of the evening, and not the singer George, either.

After all the power cuts it wasn't surprising that a few of us had pocket torches – *always be prepared*, more than one of us said, and: *I promise I will do my best*, a few others – including Cllr Simpson and Brian Wilmot – responded in a chant. *~To do my duty to God and to the Queen! ~To help other people! ~And to keep the Scout law!!* Bee caught my arm in the dark and whispered in my ear: What have we started? ~They say adversity brings out the best in the British, I whispered back. When Cllr Simpson shouted, Onwards and upwards! We shall conquer Mt Rochester! Bee whispered: The best? ~This may be as good as it gets.

At the twelfth floor a man with a leg brace said, This is me, I can't make it any further. You're welcome to stop here. A small breakaway party formed, but most of us kept going and: *~The workers! United!* Cllr Simpson chanted, possibly for the first time in his life.

At the fifteenth floor we stopped for light refreshments before the final push. Someone knocked over an empty bottle that rolled and bounced invisibly down the steps in the dark and for a while it became a game, rolling empties, trying to follow them in the weak torch beams, making bets, counting the steps, the bounces, before the inevitable crunch, and ~Fucking vandals, someone said, and *it might have been me*. ~I blame the council. There was laughter, but JJ said: Think of the crew that has to clean this up. The Leader said: Come on, gents, we're nearly there.

At the eighteenth, JJ fumbled with the unfamiliar keys, then stood by the open door, as if welcoming us to the Jellicoe family seat. ~Well, said Cllr Simpson, sinking into a wicker chair that creaked and groaned with the shock, we knocked the bastard off, and JJ said: So which of us is Tenzing Norgay?

Bee found the candles she had promised, JJ found more booze and dug out the battery-powered Philips record player I'd always laughed at and he always said was better than a

Dansette. So there was music – not loud music, not by the standards of 1972, when the sound rigs of rock bands were higher than the tower we'd just climbed, but it was audible, just about – and there was candle light and beer and wine and, within minutes, marijuana. It was a party, much like any other party you ever went to in those days, and when I talked to the people who lived there, to Bee and JJ's neighbours, who'd just moved back in, they were delighted, the council had done a marvelous job, they said. ~And the builders? ~Well, I guess you'd say the builders have made amends, they said. Wouldn't have chosen them again, myself, I was a bit shocked, to tell the truth, when I heard, but I've got to say they've really come up trumps. I lapped it up as long as I decently could before letting them know who I was – they'd mostly assumed they were talking to JJ – and calling Brian over to meet his new fans.

I shared a joint with Cllr Simpson, who had mercifully ditched the safari jacket, less mercifully revealing a pus-coloured nylon shirt with a pattern of fanciful 1920s cars printed all over it, all swooping running boards, Tommy guns and molls in cloche hats at the wheel, and we both knew – surely? – that he was far too old to be the man he was impersonating? We were forty, JJ – *we* were far too old – but he must have had a couple of decades on us, and when I inhaled hard and held my breath and the cars on his shirt began to move under their own steam, it was time to move on and refill my glass.

Bee was high, too, not smoking high, necessarily, though maybe that as well. She'd been getting the same adoration all day from those who knew how important the tenants association had been, how important she had been, to the way things had turned out. Because it was all about the money, when you got down to it. The moolah. Dollars. Dinero. It doesn't matter who you employ: spend more, you'll get a better building, I'd said. JJ had blanched at first, Cllr Simpson, too, but Cllr Easton knew what I was talking about. ~Get this wrong and we'll lose any faith people ever had that we could make things better. ~We'll lose hope. ~We'll lose the New Jerusalem.

It made no sense to quibble, and in the end we spent more rebuilding and refurbishing the Rochester Estate than we had putting it up in the first place, but what did that matter? It wasn't our money, Wilmots' money, except for the management fee we sliced off the top. The more we spent the more we made, the happier everybody was, so –

Bee was delighted. Now she'd won, too.

Even JJ looked happy. Not happy enough, or drunk or stoned enough to join in when Cllr Simpson tried to lead a chorus of 'Lily the Pink', of course, but he stood in the kitchen sipping beer from a can, deflecting the praise and congratulations of his neighbours with unpractised grace. He knew he deserved it. I'll give him that. He came in to the living room and watched Bee dance and he looked like he deserved that, too. He was a man at home, for once, in a home he had built surrounded by the people he'd built it for, and his wife was far and away the most beautiful person in the room.

I danced with Frances, and drank whisky with Philip. I danced in the general direction of the young man who had come with Cllr Easton. He had exquisite curly black hair, the tightest Wranglers I had ever seen and buttocks like a pair of shrink-wrapped grapefruit – *no, not* like: *they were* sui generis, *his buttocks* – and his throat was so pale, so slender, and the way his black hair curled against it made me want to kiss him there and then, but still he was no George. ~Hi, I said, my name's JJ, and *it could have been.* Ten minutes is all it took. Ten more minutes in our mother's womb is all there is between us. I could have been you.

I could have had what you have had.

I danced with Philip and drank vodka with Frances.

Philip pretended to find me amusing. Cllr Easton caught me coming out of the toilet, and it really felt like being caught. ~I've been chatting to that chap, he said, gripping my arm with one hand and pointing through the hall doorway with the other, to where Philip was now dancing to Conway Twitty with a woman in purple hot pants, What's he doing here? ~He's JJ's . . . he's married to our niece. ~You're married to the Flying Squad? ~Well, distantly. At one or two removes. ~Still . . . he relaxed his grip on my elbow, that's interesting. ~It is, I agreed. I couldn't quite work out how it had come about myself.

Bee waved someone off from the front door and pulled me away from Cllr Easton, into the smaller of the two bedrooms, still big enough for a couple of single beds, one against each wall, a single candle on the windowsill. It would have been the Williams children's room, I imagined. They would have been six and four. These weren't Gwyneth and David's beds, though, these beds here now, piled high with coats, these were just guest beds, in a spare room where Bee threw her arms around my neck and said: We did it! ~We did. ~You and me, Charlie. We did it. I stepped back a pace. ~There were a few others involved, I said. ~Forget them, Charlie. You know what I mean.

I did. We hadn't agreed. She'd hated me, it was my fault, Wilmots' fault, we'd come at it from different ends, but, in the end, we'd wanted the same thing, and it was JJ's fault, not mine, and it was her and me – without us this thing we both wanted, whatever we wanted it for, would never have happened, and it was JJ's fault, and we got it, we did it, this block, this flat, this room, these beds were proof of that. It was us. She chucked the coats from one of the beds onto the pile on the other, ignoring those that slid to the floor, and sat down. She pulled me down to sit beside her. ~Are you all right about it, I said. Living here? She nodded. I reached across and lifted her face. ~Chin up, soldier. ~No, really – *don't say really* – it was my idea. ~That's not what JJ says. ~Of course not. But we agreed. I told him if he was going to do penance, he might as well do it properly. ~And you? ~I've got what I want. For now. ~And you're happy? ~I'm delirious, and I kissed her. I mean, I really did aim for the cheek, as perhaps she had earlier, but, somehow, she turned her head and she pulled me backwards onto the bed, or I lost my balance and toppled her, or – who knows? – the point is, we were lying on the bed, a single bed, necessarily close, and then she was sitting up again, pulling her dress over her head and lying down, and pulling me down, unbuttoning my shirt, and her chest looked *flat* her breasts splayed where she lay back, her stomach smooth and soft but still resistant to pressure, to my lips, like meat, like uncooked liver – *not like liver, what am I thinking of? like* – it doesn't matter, the point was not what her flesh was like, but what it wasn't like, that it was and wasn't what I was accustomed to. Her pubic hair was pubic hair like any other. Similes pretend to make things equal but really only emphasize the difference because *to be similar is precisely not to be identical*, I am not you, although I could have been, for her then, did it feel any different? Could I have been you? In the dark? *What difference could it make?*

She said: Are you going down there? ~I will if you will. And we did. And it was not so different after all, the thighs clamped around my face were smoother than I was used to, she didn't put her fingers in my arse, let alone her tongue, and when I tried to get at hers she clenched her buttocks so tight I doubt she shat for a week, but – despite all the drinks and the drugs and not having slept for months and even though I'm no expert and it was 1972 and the female orgasm had only recently been invented – I'm sure she came too, more than once, and

the power came back on, then. The lights burned our eyes and scorched our naked flesh, and

there was a general, communal, multi-throated roar from the living room, topped only by the bellowing voice of Cllr Simpson: Turn everything on! Turn it on! *Up the miners!*

This South African concoction, which I refuse to dignify with the name of brandy, is not only filthy but practically non-alcoholic, too. Twenty percent: what's that? More sherry than spirit. Fortified wine – vile phrase! It is sweet and clings to the palate like peanut butter. The gold flakes may look pretty to a six year-old, and may be harmless to the digestion, but they have no place in my diet. I can't drink it. And yet. And yet and yet – there is nothing else here, in the flat, and I have not yet written my speech for the morning.

There is tea, I suppose, but it is three a.m. No time for tea, or coffee. They say – *who says?* Bee always used to say, but these days the answer is obvious: Wikipedia says – Balzac drank eighty cups of coffee a day, which – even allowing for the diminutive capacity of nineteenth-century crockery – must have been a bit of a challenge for the poor man's kidneys, but never seemed to inhibit his ability to get words on paper.

I don't want coffee. Or tea.

There's a twenty-four hour supermarket just off Rye Lane, and another on the Old Kent Road and these days probably plenty more I don't know about, but I know those two.

Peckham's nearer, the Old Kent Road easier to navigate – the pavements are broader and for the most part less uneven – but I'll go to Peckham, all the same. There'll be no fucker around to get in my way this time of night, and the scooter is more than a match for the council's attempts to turn the route into an obstacle course.

The Easy Rider. Diana took one look and used the words *mid-life crisis* – as if I were going to live to a hundred and sixty! She said, You know what I mean, and I did. I just didn't care. She said, Who do you think you are, the Leader of the Pack? And I remembered then: Vroom, vroom. I said, The Shangri-Las, I said. And that's what I remembered then. Because she was, wasn't she? Diana. Going out with a him. Though she wasn't still at school, she was working but that wasn't where she met him. They met at night school. Angela wasn't letting her off any easier than us, was she JJ, just because she was a girl? She was going to have a decent job, an office job with some respect, a job that made a difference, made her different, even if it started with shorthand. And she met him there, the young lad with the bike. And he was a good lad, too, a decent kid despite the leathers, Angela said, he was going to change the world, they would change the world together (just like you and me, JJ, just like you and me) but getting caught between a builder's truck and the back end of the number 12 soon put a stop to that. What could we do? Not that it was our problem. Diana had always been the one getting under our feet, and now she had something we couldn't really complain about her being miserable over. Which she was. Dear God, she was. No one was ever coming close to him, to her, and so they never did. And you wonder why I prefer Frances?

So when Diana objected to the Easy Rider I wasn't going

to get in to her reasons, but I wasn't going to listen to them, either. It's really called the Easy Rider, by the way, and not just by me: that's honestly the manufacturer's name. Dougie found it, helped me search online. I never knew such things existed. It's black, of course, a three-wheeler with – for a scooter – enormous chrome-rimmed wheels, chrome mud-guards, chrome mirrors, a football-sized headlamp and extended handlebars. ~You'll look like Dennis Hopper on Medicare, Dougie said, and that was good enough for me. It cost four grand, sterling – about one-sixth the price of a real Harley trike, but still a good wodge more than your average putt-about on the streets of south London. When I havered, Dougie said: Have you got the money? ~I have. ~So who d'you think you're saving it for, Uncle Charlie? The answer of course was him. And Frances, of course, his mother. Some for Diana, if I didn't manage to outlive her. They say – the manufacturers say – the battery would last thirty-one miles. Not exactly coast-to-coast, even on this tiny septic isle, but it would get me to the all-night shops and back.

I wasn't trying to recapture some lost youth – the lost youths of my youth stayed lost, and were all the better for it. I'd never been a fan of motorbikes, never had one, always preferred cars. They say – *who says?* – your first sports car is like your first love, usually inadequate, never forgotten. I would own plusher, more expensive models in my pomp, but nothing ever really topped the TR3 I bought in 1962, and might have called George, if I'd known, and been the kind of person who names inanimate objects. I never owned a bike. The only time I ever rode one – if you don't count sitting pillion on a stranger's Vespa in Rome, which is another story, and nothing really to do with motorbikes at all – was during the war. *The* war, that war. We would have been ten, I suppose, when we first saw it, when the Herefordshire farmer we'd been billeted on pointed out the ancient Royal Enfield he'd left in the barn with a lot of other rusty machinery he kept saying should be melted down for Spitfire parts, but never was. I couldn't have cared less. I didn't want to be there and I didn't want to ride a motorbike. I wanted to be in Peckham, at the Centre, swimming, roller skating, watching dancers dance. And you? You were crying yourself to sleep every night. Crying when you woke up in the morning and found it wasn't all a dream, that you were still there, with the pigs and the cows and the farmer and the farmer's family, and Mum and Dad and Angela not there, and

you're sure that was me?

I forget. *Sometimes, I forget.* There was a cockerel, of course there was, I remember that. Which was all very well, but you wanted to hear Dad shouting up the stairs in the morning, telling us to shake our lazy bones, telling us capitalism wasn't going to destroy itself, now was it? - although by 1940, by the last time we heard him say it, he couldn't have been so sure. You wanted to hear Mum saying she'd meet us at the Centre after school. And instead we got Farmer bloody Jones reminding us that pigsties didn't clean themselves. John Jones - really; *don't say really* - never got over there being another JJ in the house: even if no one ever called him that, or ever would, it tickled him all the same. But was there ever a name more boring than John Jones

or more ridiculous than Jolyon Jellicoe?

It was Hope -

I've not mentioned the girls before, have I? Should I bring them into it, tomorrow? Childhood reminiscence? I'm sure Diana would approve, provided I skip lightly across the bedtime tears.

So, Hope. The Jones' younger daughter and, for once, a child aptly named, a beam of pure energy and enthusiasm, who welcomed us to Blackbrook Farm much as an open-minded missionary's wife might have welcomed newly-converted savage children. London, our lives, our parents' views on discipline and school and the war, our accents and – above all – our identical appearance were all a source of endless, good-natured fascination. *They say what? How small? How big? Say that again. Say that again, say that again, again, again.* The thought that her life and that of everyone she'd ever met before – living up to their ears in mud and shit and talking so bloody slowly we could happily take a nap between syllables – might not be everybody else's idea of normal had clearly never struck her before. Now she would investigate the specimens she'd been granted with all the rigour of a natural scientist. JJ tolerated it, like a life model used to absorbing others' scrutiny, but I played it up, twisting my vowels into weird approximations of the way I thought the posh spoke then, telling more and more outrageous lies: JJ and I had swum with whales in the Thames, our uncle (Tony!) was a silver miner in Bolivia, teachers in London weren't allowed to hit you unless they let you hit them back. In my version of the Coronation, King George and Queen Elizabeth took time out from their busy day to join us at the Peckham Pioneer Centre: I did all the voices. Hope didn't swallow that one, but only because when we told her the truth about the Centre she assumed we must be lying anyway. A swimming pool? Dances? A gymnasium and bicycles and roller skates you could just pick up and use? In a palace made of glass? We must be lying, but she didn't mind, it was all part of the curious phenomenon of you and me, JJ, the alien beings billeted in her home by forces so far beyond her comprehension it might as well have been the will of some mischievous Greek deity. ~Are you two totally identical? ~Yes. ~Every inch? ~Every inch. (What was she talking about?) ~Do people get you mixed up? ~All the time. Teachers. Coppers. JJ's always getting clobbered for stuff I do. (In my defence, it's what she wanted to hear.) ~Like what? ~Oh, stuff. ~But what stuff?

[Pause]

~Did you ever hear of the Mitcham bank job?

She laughed and punched me, not hard, but like a boy might punch another boy to show he wasn't being had. I struck back, my hand open, more of a slap than a punch, and then we wrestled. She was older than me and much stronger, a farm girl. She sat astride my chest, pinning my arms to the ground with her knees, doing elephant feet – what we called elephant feet, I don't know what she called it – on my chest with the first two fingers of each hand, and demanding my surrender. But before I could admit defeat, JJ, who had been sitting motionless against the barn wall, watching us without a word, jumped up and hissed: Your Dad's coming! At which Hope sprang away, leaving me to scramble to my feet before either of us realized he was lying.

When, after we'd been at Blackbrook for a year, Hope told her father that JJ still wasn't happy, he suggested we try to mend the old motorbike. He said we could ride it round the farm if we could make it work. He meant us boys, but it was Hope who took the challenge to heart. She was two years older than us, her sister Faith a couple of years older still – yes, Faith, and Hope: the Joneses never got round to Charity, you said, in one of your more acerbic moments. *Or was that me?* More than likely, I suppose, but a motorcycle was a boy's thing, their father thought. For all that he never allowed them to pass a day without some form of labour on the farm, he would never let his daughters meddle with machinery, for fear, presumably, of inserting a spanner in the cosmic works and bringing the universe crashing to a halt around us. Faith got the message, but Hope's contrariety sprang eternal. Anything her family did not care for became her passion. Including us.

Was it really a year? Or is that just a figure of speech, a Biblical forty days and forty nights? It was hot again, I know that. Spring was pretty much over when we arrived, *summer i-cummen in*, the lambs on the neighbouring farms quite sturdy and not long, Hope gleefully informed us, for this world. Summer had come in and buggered off again, the bombing had started and winter arrived, with actual snow, the letters from Mum getting shorter and less frequent, our replies less frequent still, then spring again and the bombing not yet letting up and we had come full circle. So it might have been late May or even early June of 1941 when Hope spoke to her father about JJ and he spoke to us about the bike, and he might have already known about our parents and not got around to telling us. He might have been looking for the right moment; it is possible.

Oh, Diana, do I have to do this?

I don't have to. I'm eighty-five, my brother's dead. I don't have to do a damn thing I don't want to do. Ah, that's bollocks, isn't it? The sort of thing old people like to say to license our gutless egotism and make the rest of you feel bad. Isn't that the way it works? He was a good man, or at least not a bad one.

Up till then we'd played around the bike, ignoring it most of the time, like all the inexplicable abandoned heaps of rusting metal that littered the farm, but occasionally we would incorporate it into our games, Hope pretending to be a secret agent escaping Nazis far behind enemy lines, me balancing one-footed on the saddle, my other leg stretched out before me, arms aloft like a dancer, pretending to be a stunt rider. It was a prop. None of us regarded it as a machine that might ever move again, much less that we could make it happen. But Farmer Jones believed boys grew up understanding machinery the way girls understood poultry feed and needlework. He dug out the manual from a stack of books and papers in the strange, windowless room beside the pantry that seemed to have no function other than as a final repository for things no one wanted but could not quite bring themself to throw away. He said he hadn't looked at it since he bought the bike off a man in the village who'd lost both legs at Passchendaele and couldn't ride it any more. ~Never needed it, he said. It's not much, but it'll tell you what the parts are. You'll have to work out what they're *for* yourselves. That'll be fun, won't it? He handed the thick greasy manual to JJ, who thanked him politely and, as soon as we were back in the barn, handed it on to Hope.

How do you tell two boys their parents have died on the last night of the longest aerial bombing campaign the world had ever known, not because they took a direct hit, but because they lit the gas to put the kettle on?

He couldn't have known it was the last night, then.

Over the months that followed, during every break she got from school, from the farm and from her mother and her father, Hope stripped and cleaned and scoured and filed and polished and oiled and repainted every part the bike possessed. It was mostly our hands – JJ's and mine – that got dirty, while Hope hovered, trying to look as if she were just encouraging us boys, but there was no doubt in our minds whose show this was. We were just her beards, so to speak.

It was Angela who told us, in the end. She came to visit

and there was no disguising why she'd come. She returned to London, to Tony, to work – to working, of all things, in all places, in the Centre, making fighter-bomber parts for the RAF. She couldn't take us with her, she said, we were better off where we were.

He said he could spare us some petrol, he was a farmer: it was easier for him than for most people.

The day the engine first fired Hope flung her arms around our necks and kissed us both. We were eleven, she was thirteen. At the sound of the pistons turning something came alive in JJ. It was as if he'd finally accepted there was a point to all of this, that some things might be mended after all. When we fixed the clutch and worked out why the brakes weren't working, Hope taught herself to ride – slowly, around the barn – then taught us, JJ and me, so we could ride it out in the fields where her father might see us. We rode alone, and then together, us boys, JJ going first and taking to it straight away, the look of concentration on his face – eyes squeezed almost closed, the tip of his tongue caught between his teeth – giving way to increasing joy with each successful change of gear. I was more timid, more tentative – which Diana, who can't keep up with me navigating Rye Lane on my Easy Rider, now finds hard to believe. She says she knows me and I'd have flung myself at it. But this time it was JJ who threw himself into the chance to do something new, something fun. I mostly rode pillion, happy to let him explore how fast he could push us, how low into the bends, how steep the slope and broad the ditch we could jump and still come away intact, alive.

We were alive.

And through it all, Hope had to watch from the barn until one day, finally, during yet another summer, her father took her mother, who rarely left the kitchen, into Hereford for market day, for the piglets and the heifers and to see what use she could make of the clothing coupons she hadn't touched since she'd received the family's books. Hope didn't need to worry about her sister. Faith's attention was directed solely at the village, by which I mean the village pub, where the landlord's son was about to be posted to North Africa. She was not the least bit interested in Hope, or us, or our smelly, dirty motorbike. So she wasn't watching when JJ kick-started it and Hope climbed on behind and I climbed on behind her and the three of us rolled out of the barn and onto the track towards the river, Hope's arms around JJ, mine around her. We were a little cumbersome at first, but picked up speed as JJ tested the bike's power and balance with three, and found we were so small, so light, that it made little difference until Hope leaned the wrong way into a curve and we all came off together, the bike on top of us, but no one hurt, we hadn't been going any real speed, just enjoying the dappled shade of the river bank. We dusted ourselves down, stood up and rolled the bike under the largest weeping willow, the branches of which dipped into the water on one side and brushed the early summer grass on the other. We lay down again, invisible from the outside, and it was then, that afternoon, when we were twelve and Hope fourteen – not earlier, not when we first arrived – that she asked if we were identical in every inch. And it was JJ, not me, who responded: every inch. ~Prove it. ~We will if you will. Honestly, he did. You did. I went along with it, stripping off my clothes and –

Diana, Diana. Don't go getting the idea there's some primordial moment happening here, some dark, bucolic trauma that bent me out of shape and made me queer. That's not the way it works. I'm queer. I'm gay, I'm homosexual.

I'm a fairy.

I just am.

And I was then, whatever Hope did - *whatever Bee did* - whatever I did, and afterwards she said there was one way she could tell us apart now, after all.

Is it possible to be drunk in charge of a mobility scooter? It is, I know it is, empirically. But what I mean is - is it an offence? Could I be apprehended, charged and prosecuted for what I am about to do? It's hard to move around here without encountering the forces of law and order. My route takes me right past Peckham police station. Fuck 'em. I dare say it's an offence, but I'm eighty-five and I'm going to do it anyway. You'd hope Peckham's finest would have better things to do than arresting old men trundling through the streets at six-and-a-half mph.

I lever myself to my feet and make it down the spiral stair without mishap. That South African abomination must really be as weak as nun's piss, after all: even the twenty percent is probably a lie. Slowly, deliberately, like everything else I do these days, I open the front door and roll the Easy Rider past Mrs. Vega's door before I strap my trusty knobkerrie in place and clamber aboard with all the elegance and dignity of a colonial major's wife mounting an elephant for the first time, and - *we're off!* - as far as the electronic gates, which open at my remote command more slowly even than the camel squeezing itself through the needle's eye. I live, as JJ liked to remind me, in a literal gated community. There were gates here in the 30's, I remind him, too. Reminded him. When it was the Centre. Not electronic gates, of course, but gates all the same, guarded by Baldie Hayes, who was sharp enough to tell us apart, which is more than a motion sensor can do. Anyone who lived near enough could join, but you had to *join*, it wasn't a free-for-all. You had to be a member; you had to pay.

Because these things cost money, they said, and couldn't run themselves

plus it kept the riff-raff out

the Biologists said, because the working classes were all very well – all very unwell, as it turned out – but we only want the respectable ones, for this experiment. It was an old argument, as old as socialism, and JJ's right, they were never socialists, but that wasn't ever my point. Outside, now, turn right; listen for the gates grinding shut behind me

to keep the riff-raff out.

At the corner of Queen's Road a row of villas set back from the pavement offers a touch of misplaced antebellum charm, all iron filigree over balconies draped in wisteria, and there, in the windows of one, I can see four or five Vote Labour posters, red bleached to pale brown in the sodium city glow of three a.m. On the opposite side of the road, in a new-build block on a small infill site, I know there is a Conservative poster, just one. Last time, the Tories lost here by twenty-five thousand votes; tomorrow, I dare say it will be more. Who on earth, in that cramped and shoddily constructed flat, could feel the need to proclaim themselves so out of step with an indifferent neighbourhood? There are no UKIP posters – there is no UKIP candidate – their job being done, although not too well round here, where three-quarters of the population voted last year to Remain

but not you

no, not me – we would cancel each other out, you and me. Unlike the sole Tory, however, I kept my intentions to myself. No one in the Centre would have voted Leave just because I put a poster in my window, and it would only have upset Mrs. Vega. It had been so much easier in 1975. The party line was clear, my party. *The Morning Star* was the only paper wanting out, but you have to remember most of the Labour Party did, too, and a big chunk of the Cabinet

and Enoch Powell

and Enoch Powell – him again, that man again. I admit it wasn't easy, finding myself on the same side, after all those years, but that didn't mean we were wrong, that he was wrong, on that, whatever his motives. I don't see anyone today refusing contraception because it was Enoch Powell who let women have the Pill. Sometimes you can't choose your allies. When you get down to it, the EU still has the only constitution in the world committed to capitalism. Tony Benn said that in 1975. Ask the Greeks if he was wrong.

I know. I know.

I know you voted Remain, and – I *won't say a word.* Tomorrow. Not a word about Europe. Not a fucking word. In the morning I'll get up, again, and I'll vote, again, I'll go to your funeral and keep my mouth shut about Europe. No one wants to know.

During the day, even though there's more traffic, I drive my Easy Rider on the roads, because the pavements are impossibly crowded, especially around the bus stops, where they're basically just scrums and no one moves until you run over their feet, which doesn't always end well. At this time of night the pavements are almost empty, though there's more traffic than you might expect, driven more recklessly than daytime congestion allows: night buses, minicabs and shiny high-performance cars with tinted windows throbbing to bass-heavy sound systems; mopeds with outsized pizza-delivery boxes bungeed to the pillion, or faster, newer models ridden two-up, weaving in and out between the pavements and the roadway, looking for opportunities, for civilian cars stopped at the lights, for drunken women, or old men on mobility scooters, perhaps, the latter rare as hen's teeth at four in the morning but – luckily for me – just as worthless in their eyes. Heading west under the railway bridge I'm pleased to hear that I was right about the police. There's a helicopter clattering low in the orange sky, circling the flats of Cossall Park. There's something about the visceral noise of rotor blades at close quarters, however often you hear it – and round here that means most days – something that makes your heart beat a little faster. I know this is hyperbolic, a second-hand cinematic anxiety. I know I'm not in the middle of a riot – not now, *not for years* – I know I'm not clinging to a roof in Saigon or rushing through Henry Hill's final, busy dealing day. But I feel it all the same. The world's fundamental divide, I'm sure, is not between the queer and the straight, male and female, black and white, or even rich and poor – although all of those play into it. It is between those who find the force of law and order reassuring, however subconsciously, and those of us for whom it is a threat.

There are no election posters here.

At the bus garage, the stands are empty. Behind them, Morrison's car park is empty, too, or almost. It is empty of cars. I breeze past, revving the Easy Rider. I hang a left into Rye Lane, sticking to the pavement, against the one way, and there's the Poundshop, pawn shop, SuperDrug – never as much fun as it sounds – a bookies, Halifax, Vodaphone. You'll know the drill, wherever you live. Then cavernous grocers' shops that, sixteen hours a day, sell okra, sweet potato, six varieties of chilli, skinny chickens with the feet still on and dull-eyed tilapia by the crate. Plus – always – phonecards, countless phonecards. *Call Nigeria for 1p/min.* Now, though, they are shuttered and tagged, the swollen, bursting letters illegible up close, or papered over with posters advertising club nights, festivals or God. Jesus is big round here. The election doesn't get a look-in.

I turn right and tether my steed to the hitching-post.

~There you go, boss. Contactless? – and I think: *I may be.* It's a family store, I've seen this kid grow up, grow into the job, even though I don't know his name, and he doesn't know mine. I doubt contactless would cover the bottle I've asked him to fetch down from the highest shelf behind the counter, one of the random treasures you can find here, where the quality of the stock varies with fire-sales and suppliers' arrests, and the prices correlate to nothing at all. This time they're asking £37, preposterously little for a cognac of this pedigree. I offer cash and the young man looks surprised. ~Bag? he says. I agree it would be easier. In the event, the tremor in my left hand makes it hard to thread my rigidly curled fingers through the plastic handles he holds out; together, though, we manage it. I turn, and behind me a huge West African, as broad as a small truck, holds out a tube of sour cream and onion Pringles that bizarrely matches his fancy gold-and-green agbada. There is no way we can pass in the narrow aisle between the till and the door. He inclines his head slightly, almost a bow, and steps back, treading on the toes of a skinny white girl, one of a gaggle of Goldsmiths students, I would guess, or the art college at Camberwell, their arms cradling a month's supply of milk and chocolate HobNobs. She squeals and the African apologizes. She says it's no problem, yeah? No one seems to think it is a question.

Outside again, I slot the bottle into the seat-back pocket – the Easy Rider's lack of a proper shopping basket being the minor tax convenience pays to style – strap on my stick and head for home. The helicopter has gone for now. Just beyond the police station, on the way past the enormous building site that has been empty since I can't remember when, I reach eight mph, as advertised. Then nine, then ten, and, as I swing into St Mary's Road, I find myself barrelling towards a fox, its yellow eyes twin lamps in the glare, luring me towards the rocks, not away, and I discover that, difficult as it is to capsize a tricycle, it is not impossible. The fox slinks aside, the Easy Rider ploughs into the kerb and I am thrown - I *fall* - onto the tarmac between two parked cars. The bottle rolls clear, too, miraculously unbroken. That word again. As I confirm this, a large, dark shape looms over me, blocking out the streetlamp's glow. It is a man, a young man in a track-suit, hood pulled up against the pre-dawn chill. He has a dog, a bull terrier, on a heavy chain. Across the road, two or three more figures are watching, waiting. ~You okay, bruv? I nod. I'm eighty-five. Stabbed for a bottle of cognac he won't appreciate. No way to go. He rights the Easy Rider. ~Cool scooter. You sure you're okay? I nod again, and he helps me to my feet. I am scraped and scuffed and I will hurt like hell if I stop long enough to think about it, but nothing is broken. ~You need to go to hospital, yeah. I'm not sure if it's a ques-tion, but I tell him no, I'll be fine, if he could just help me back onto my scooter. Which he does. And everything seems to work. I thank him and resume my journey. I'm almost home, almost at the gates when I hear him laugh and call after me:

~Mad old cunt, yeah?

I've had worse.

Back in the flat I pour myself a drink. The polling stations will open in three hours.

~We should - we should not - have done that. ~We shouldn't, I said. I'm queer. ~More to the point, Bee said, looking at me sideways, you're his brother. ~More to the point? ~You know what I mean.

What did she mean? That I was less important than her marriage? That my being gay wasn't that big a deal, not even to myself? That I could have been you?

~I could have been him, I said, in the dark. How would you have known the difference?

To be similar is not to be identical. But that, of course, is what we were.

She laughed. ~He never did that.

I was shocked. ~Never?

~And anyway, she said, I don't think you can be entirely . . . ~Entirely what? ~Entirely that way. We're here, aren't we? ~We've agreed we shouldn't be. ~I saw the way you looked at Georgina at the party, like some old roué hanging around the stage door. ~You mean George? She smiled: Exactly.

I think I must have realized then, realized that – the way she'd looked at George, too. Georgina. I laughed. I caught her eye and, naked, she blushed, then hit me with a pillow and I caught her arms, and we held each other off, for a moment, our arms equally rigid, locked together, our hands grasping at each others' elbows until we relaxed and kissed and

kissed and kissed, like brother and sister, until I sat up and quoted Rochester: *And the best kiss was the deciding lot*, I said, and together we chanted: *Whether the boy fucked you or I the boy.*

George. Georgina.

We stopped, and

we began reaching for our clothes. ~Oh, God, Charlie. This never happened.

Of course it never happened.

I'm eighty-five. It was 1972. Who's going to trust my

memory? *Like brother and sister*, for example. Did I just say that? Angela would be pissing herself, and not for the usual reasons. She kissed us, sure, our sister. When we came back from Herefordshire, she met us on the platform at Paddington, with Tony in tow. She threw her arms around our shoulders, pulled us into her bosom – it was definitely a bosom, even then – and kissed the tops of our heads. We were going on fourteen, she was still a couple of inches taller than us. I remember that – I remember – Bee. I remember what we did.

I remember we dressed and returned to the party, her first, me a few minutes later. We were being careful. There was no reason for you to know, and every reason why you shouldn't and I kept out of your way – their way, Bee and JJ's way – after that. The party broke up fairly soon, anyway. Peter drove me home, saying how much he'd enjoyed himself, how enlightening he'd found Cllr Simpson's opinions on the Common Market and how entertaining my nephew Philip had been – such an interesting job! I avoided JJ, avoided Bee – avoided you both – for some months, which wasn't hard, to begin with, because the Rochester Estate was all over for me bar the billing, which wasn't anything I needed to talk to you about. We both had other people for that. And once the invoices were agreed, and the slow mills of the finance department could be left to grind Wilmots' remuneration exceeding small, I asked Brian to let me oversee a shopping precinct deal in Loughborough that looked like it might be going pear-shaped. ~Are you sure? ~A change of air will do me good. ~It's Loughborough, Charlie, not Biarritz.

Nixon went to China, the miners went back twenty per cent better off, and I went to Leicestershire. After that, a couple of tower blocks in Paisley and a couple more in Stoke-on-Trent, an office block in Colchester – *I get around* – it was a pilgrimage, not quite necessary as far as Wilmots' business went. As Brian kept pointing out, there were better things I could be doing with my time, more profitable things, but the point of penitence is surely, pointlessness. ~What on earth do you feel guilty about? he asked. ~What have you got? I said.

Did I feel guilty?

I was guilty. It made no difference how I felt.

And Bee?

I had no idea how Bee felt, because *we'd agreed it never happened.*

By the time I came up for air, Poulson's bankruptcy dealings had been passed to the Met, there were statements in the House and Reggie Maudling had resigned. (Prime Ministers are easy, but Home Secretaries? Amber Rudd, Theresa May, someone Labour. Alan Johnson? There's a reason the doctors never ask. Maudling, Callaghan, Jenkins, no idea. Not a chance.)

I called JJ, and we met - at a bar in the Festival Hall. Bee was there, quite like old times. She said: Hello, stranger. ~Sorry, I've been busy. ~Too busy for family? I asked JJ if he'd heard from Angela at all. ~She's in hospital. ~Oh. Right. How is she? ~Very nearly dead, it's nice of you to ask. ~It's not the first time, I said. It won't be the last. ~It might, he said. And eventually, it will.

It was, we just didn't know it then.

~How's Diana? I asked, because I thought I should. ~Tearing her hair out, Bee answered for you. As I say, quite like old times. ~Frances and Phil? Frances hadn't been born when we came back from Herefordshire, you had us to yourself for a couple of years, didn't you, Diana? Then, Frances was there and tiny - *for six months she cried every time I picked her up. She didn't do that to you. We were identical, but she could tell the difference. And then, one day, she didn't. Not when I cuddled her, or gave her a bottle, and she loved me, I swear she did. Her love was fierce, even then.* There was a reason I was asking about Philip, though, a reason I hoped JJ would pick up on and Bee might not. She didn't. ~Well, now you two have caught up on the family news, she said, shall I get us all another drink?

With Bee at the bar, there was only JJ to talk to, or to talk to me, so we watched the people flow around us. Men in suits, in corduroy jackets, in bell-bottomed denim and floral printed shirts. Women in trouser suits or mini-skirts or floor-length cotton dresses, their hair in Elnet-spray headsets or long and loose, held back from their faces by delicate bands around their foreheads. A population looking backwards, looking forwards, looking inward, no longer knowing what was wanted. Had we ever known? Of course we had. In 1968 we had. Four years ago – *fifty years ago* – we had. And no, we never had. We thought we wanted more, that's all.

More what?

More fun. More sex, more love, more money, more freedom, more law – more laws about freedom – more drugs, more music, more television, more doctors, more nurses, more taxes, more football, more houses. Just . . . more. *More! More! Is the cry of a mistaken soul*, Blake said – William Blake (who saw an angel up a tree on Peckham Rye and was briefly fashionable at the time), *Less than All cannot satisfy Man.*

Or Woman. Or Pansy.

JJ said, How's business?

We were almost fourteen but she was taller than us, still, when she kissed the tops of our heads, like a sister, like a mother, while Tony stepped forward, reaching for my cardboard suitcase, and I shook his hand. He laughed. ~Proper little gent, he said, aren't you, JJ? ~That's Charlie, Angela said, but only because she could see you giggling into your fist. On the bus, Tony stowed our suitcases in the space under the stairs and Angela wouldn't let us leave them to go up top, so we sat on the bench seats with our backs to the windows - me and JJ one side, Angela and Tony the other - facing each other across the aisle. After a couple of minutes, JJ and I turned and knelt up on the seats so we could see out. ~It's so busy! JJ said. ~We've been stuck on a farm for four years. What did you expect? But I knew what he expected. Everything flattened, bombed to rubble, maybe an occasional survivor crawling from the wreckage, blood trickling from his wounds. Stray dogs gnawing faceless carcasses. Winston Churchill in a hat and pinstripe suit astride the debris, cigar in mouth, and a Tommy gun in his hands. There was some of that, of course - the rubble, I mean, not the bodies or Winnie, who by then had already lost the election and wasn't even PM any more - but less than I'd imagined. We knew the Blitz had ended years before, the V1s and V2s had petered out. We knew the worst of the bombing had been around the docks and south of the river, where we were going - not here, in the West End. We'd seen the newsreels when, a couple of times a year, Farmer Jones took us and Hope - and Faith, when she wasn't sulking - to the Ritz in Hereford. We knew life had carried on. But knowing a thing and seeing it are different. What were all these buses doing here? These cars, these people? Some were in uniform, but plenty weren't. ~Getting in our way, said Angela, that's what they're doing.

We changed buses at the Elephant & Castle. ~That's more like it, Tony said. He meant we were on home turf, but it was more what we'd expected, too. Still plenty of people - more, if anything, than on the Edgware Road – but also more destruction. Some of the bombed-out buildings had been half-heartedly fenced off; others were exposed like a beggar's sores. What we hadn't dreamed of was the riot of colour, the mass of purple flowers that pushed through the cracks and softened the edges of the broken masonry. The newsreels had been black and white. ~Bombweed, it's everywhere. ~Rosebay willowherb, JJ said, and the rest of us stared at him as if he'd sprouted flowers himself. ~Hope told me. ~Oh, *Hope* is it? Tony said. Spill the beans. Has young Charlie been in love? ~Shut up, Tony, said Angela, that's JJ, and *thank God that prick won't be there tomorrow*. I mean, I'm sorry, Diana, I know he's your dad and everything – and Frances', of course – but honestly, apart from that: was that man not a total waste of all the air he ever breathed? Honestly? Back in Peckham, he showed us the half a house we'd all be sharing, showed us around as if it hadn't been Angela who found it, who persuaded the landlord to let them have it and who paid most of the rent. Tony had discovered flat feet in 1940 and had been an anti-aircraft gunner, he said, some of the time. ~Spotter, Angela corrected. No wonder so many of the fuckers got through. Now he was a dealer, Tony said, a buyer and a seller. Which mostly meant hanging around the kitchen all day, angling for cups of tea we didn't have, and hanging around the Prince all night. JJ and I tossed a ha'penny to pick beds and chucked our few clothes in the same cupboard. ~Let's have a drink, said Angela. To celebrate. A couple of weeks later it was our birthday, and we were celebrating again. One of Tony's few actual deals had produced a bottle of sweet sparkling wine. We were fourteen, and you – you'd have been, what Diana? Two? Three? Talking, anyway, I remember that, not making any sense. ~Happy Birthday,

Angela said, sticking to the gin. We'll have to get you back to school in September. ~You don't want to go to school, do you? Tony said. You could work for me. Angela laughed. ~Doing what? ~You know, errands and that. Messages. They'd be gophers. Start at the bottom, of course. ~And work their way down?

That's when Angela's campaign to move to Bromley began in earnest. We said we'd had enough of the country, and she said: not country country, Bromley. I said we'd been to Bromley, remember? That's where the Centre's farm was. We'd spent the summer of 1938 scything shit there and JJ had almost cut his leg off. ~There'd be more space, she said. And schools. You could go to a decent school. We could have a garden. Now Tony laughed. ~What do you want with a garden? You can't grow gin. ~Ha bloody ha, said Angela. He had a point, though. Can you imagine your mother, Diana, mulching the herbaceous borders, deadheading roses?

We never got out of Peckham, not then, and I for one was glad. When the munitions factory closed, Angela got a job in a bakery. It meant early starts, while the rest of us stayed in bed; it meant hot, hard work that brought her home tired and thirsty in the early afternoons, but at least she was around when JJ and I got back from school. Tony was often around, too, though not always out of bed, or dressed. Yes, we went to school, to Addey & Stanhope down in Deptford, which wasn't far but farther than we could have gone. Angela chose the place, persuaded them to take us in, somehow bought us the shit-brown uniform Tony said he could get cheap, but couldn't when it came to it. We would walk – there were a thousand buses to steal a ride on, but mostly we walked – down the New Cross Road, past the crater that used to be Woolworths until it caught one of the last V2s, past the station and the town hall: there was always plenty to see. At school they asked us why we smelled of pig shit, why we talked so slow. We didn't, surely? But it wouldn't be the last time I'd be asked why I talk the way I do. All my life, my working life, but also my private life, my – for want of a better word – *love life*, I've been asked the same question, and it's usually been some kind of threat. I mean, don't know about you, JJ, you had the edges rounded off at UCL, but I got asked a lot, and when I did I didn't always answer, or when I answered, didn't always waste time with the truth. Which would probably have been a mixture of Dad and Mum and Manny Levinson and Hope and Angela; and the Left Book Club, the RAF, and poetry – Rochester, of course – and Bee; sleeping with educated men, and stealing books from those who didn't give me them; the Party bookshop, Lawrence & Wishart, Allen Unwin's penguins; Sartre and Sillitoe and Henry Miller and Arthur Miller and D.H. Lawrence and Trollope and Oscar Wilde and Wodehouse, and anything else I could get my hands on – in school, in barracks, in digs in Coventry and Leicester and Plymouth and Aber-fucking-deen. And what was I looking for in all those words? Myself? Hardly. I had enough trouble keeping out of my own way in real life. But the words they left me with, the voice, the blended, demented vocabulary, the neither here nor there, not fish nor fowl? Not Cocker-ney. Gaw blimey no, guvnor, not bleedin' likely, or not without a reason. What I learned – learned is the wrong word – what I *absorbed* over the years was the power to blend in, to talk comfortably with businessmen and brickies, whores and politicians, and to sound exactly like they wanted me to sound. Which is to say, not like them, exactly – imitation not being the sincerest form of flattery, after all, or not received as such, all too often, but as taking the piss – but, then again, not *too* unlike them, either. A man they could trust, do business with, or fuck.

Though not one they could love.

Since the factory closed at the end of the war, there'd been a growing campaign to get the Centre going again, to re-start the Peckham Experiment, but the Government still controlled the building. By the time we came back, JJ and me, the locals who weren't dead or stuck overseas had been holding public meetings, raising cash. They tracked the doctors down, and invited them back. They organized a petition and delivered a copy to every single MP the day the new Parliament opened, which was pretty bloody impressive, you had to admit. Dad might have appreciated that – there were two new communist MPs that year, after all – even if he disapproved of the cause. Tony thought he could see opportunities – they'd have to refurbish the place, after all – but Angela just wasn't interested. She'd never much liked the Centre or its Biologists – busy-bodies, she said – and since then she'd spent most of the war in that bloody building, she said, scared to death every day that she'd get blown to kingdom come, and she wasn't going back there if she didn't have to. And no, we couldn't join. You have to be a family, she said. We're not a bloody family. ~We *are* a family, JJ said. ~Not to them, she said. To them a family's a mum and dad and children. *Normal* children, she said, and even then I felt the way her fierce loyalty could slide into sly mockery, from where it was just a short hop to good old-fashioned disgust.

She couldn't stop us going to the re-opening party, though, a couple of weeks after the petition. Somehow, the place was still in one piece, the glass roof intact, but inside it was a shambles. The cork floors were thick with oil and grease, the gymnasium scarred by the workbenches and heavy machinery

138

it had housed. Worst of all, the swimming pool had been filled with concrete. Volunteers spent ten days hacking it out with pickaxes and shovels. The glass surround was gone, but on the day of the party, the pool was re-filled with water for the very first time. ~We should have brought our trunks, JJ said. ~What trunks?

There were sandwiches and cakes, after a fashion, the best anyone could do at the time, lemonade and – above all – beer. Tony found us in the Long Room and slipped us a couple of bottles. JJ peered at his, and at Tony, dubiously. I said, I thought you weren't coming? ~That's your sister, JJ. Me, I wouldn't miss it for the world. ~Why not, Uncle Tony? ~I'm not your uncle, he said, but he winked at me and handed over another bottle. Let's just say I do my bit for the community, shall we? I expected the beer to taste foul, but it didn't. I drank both bottles while JJ sipped at his as if expecting something to crawl out and bite him on the tongue.

Exploring the old rooms I found a piano that had been there since before the war, and tried to pick out a tune. ~What's that you're playing? It was Dr. Williamson. He smiled and put his hand on the top of the piano. ~Nothing, sir. He shook his head. ~You're not at school now . . . JJ, isn't it? I was so gobsmacked that he had any idea who I was, among all these people, after all this time – even if he was wrong – that I didn't put him straight. Besides, with the doctors, you never knew. It couldn't hurt to keep them guessing. After all, I could have been you.

Later, when the band got going, they played Glenn Miller and Louis Jordan swing numbers and some of the grown-ups tried to jitterbug, and some of them could even do it. JJ had overcome his fear, drunk three or four more bottles, and found beer *was* poisonous, after all. He was lying on his back outside

talking to no one about stars. I certainly hadn't been listening.
A girl called Rachel we both knew from junior school asked
me if I thought he'd be all right. She lived at the other end of
Dennett's Road, had been evacuated to Devon, hated it, and
came back home in 1941. Hadn't been to school since. Wasn't
the war bloody marvelous? Gawd knows what happens now. I
said JJ would be fine, and we went back indoors together. She
pulled me into the throng of enthusiastic dancers and clung on
tight. She wore a coarse and too-large cotton dress I guessed
might have been her mother's. Under it, her body felt curious-
ly soft in parts – her belly, her puppyish breasts – but lanky,
newly grown and under-fed in others. After a few minutes,
she gave up. ~You're a rubbish dancer, she said. But she was
laughing and I could see she meant no harm. I said I'd never
danced before. Like all real truths, it contained the germ of a
lie. One night after we'd got the motorbike up and running,
the girls had tried to teach us. Faith gamely marched me about
in something resembling a waltz, while Hope wrapped herself
around JJ like a poultice. Then they tried to show us some
country dancing nonsense you really need a whole barn-full
of people to do at all. There'd been another chance on VE
Day, but I kept well out of the way, looking for a friend I'd
made from a neighbouring farm, half hoping not to find him,
but not at all sure why. Now I said I didn't mind if Rachel
wanted to find someone else to dance with. She looked at me
oddly. ~Why would you mind?

Later, I saw her dancing with a grown-up, a man with a
pencil-thin moustache and a boxy, double-breasted suit who
never stopped smoking, even when he swung her into the air.

~I could show you how to do that. If you like.

The voice came from behind me. I'd been leaning against
one of the many pillars in the Long Room – *hiding behind*

it? - watching the dancers, all the dancers, not Rachel in particular, watching the band, watching the band leader, a plumber-cum-ARW from Camberwell who played the alto sax and adopted a southern coon accent for 'Is You Is, Or Is You Ain't My Baby?' It should have been excruciating, but it wasn't, not then. There were no black people in the room. Peckham in those days - and certainly the Centre - was so white I don't suppose I even knew that it was white at all. I was fourteen. ~*I could show you how to dance like that.* He was a couple of years older, this boy who had materialized behind me, a couple of inches taller, too, at least as tall as Angela. ~I can't dance, I said. I tried. ~I saw you. Had he been watching me? Or was a boy dancing so badly just impossible to miss? ~You had the wrong teacher, he said. I turned to look at him while he remained resolutely facing the dance floor, watching the adult couples and the handful of children trying to imitate them, or, the younger ones, playing a game that involved crossing the room from end to end as fast as possible, weaving and dodging the grown-ups as they whirled and spun. It was a game JJ and I had played when we were little, before the war. A shank of black hair curled down over his left eye. A soot-soft frost of newborn whiskers rimed his jaw and upper lip. He put his hand on my elbow and started to guide me out, away from the pillar. I tugged back, gesturing towards the dancers, the adults. ~They won't care. Not tonight. We're kids. Everybody's having a good time. I let myself be led. He said, I'll be the man, and - I didn't really know what he meant. He put his hand on my back, just above the waistband of my shorts, held my left hand out to one side in his right, then pushed us off, like a skater taking to the ice.

The band was all white. The dancers were white.

~What's your name? he asked during a break between numbers, and something made me say:

~JJ. What's yours?

And he said:

~George.

It was almost a year later that the police arrested John Garlick Poulson. A few months after that, they took T. Dan Smith, as well. Thomas Daniel: perfectly ordinary names, like most crooks, I think you'll find. It was October 1973, sandwiched between the Yom Kippur War and Princess Anne's wedding, and – if you're wondering how I remember that, Diana, I'm not bloody likely to forget, am I, your mother not long dead, and where it led – the arrest, I mean, not your mother – which was just the jolliest mistaken-identity story ever. Shall I use that tomorrow? Shall I? Perhaps not.

I pour another brandy, and even though this stuff is so much better than the bilge Mrs. Vega so kindly carried home for me, it doesn't make much difference. I can't seem to get drunk these days, which is probably just as well, although they say – *who says?* – it can be a bad sign, and – Frances, you must remember your uncle was arrested, too? No? Really? – *Don't* – ask your husband, Philip, he'll tell you: there was no real surprise, the scandal had broken the year before. Bankruptcy hearings, statements in the House, Reggie Maudling's resignation. You'd have to have been living at the South Pole not to know there was something going on, even if you didn't follow the ins and outs. Poulson must've been expecting a hand on his collar every morning. God knows, the rest of us did. Smith had been charged with corruption before, but got off. Now Peter – *who else?* – told Brian and me a few days before it happened that he was going to be arrested a second time. Prepare for the worst, Peter said, but hope for the best, and – *hope?* – I think it was the only time I ever heard him use the word.

I told JJ later that night, at Rochester House, but it was Bee, as usual, who answered: You said you had nothing to do with them. ~We don't. ~So what's the problem? And I had to say she had me there. ~There are certain . . . similarities. Like me, JJ was sitting at the kitchen table, staring into a glass of whisky from the bottle I'd brought and taken care to pour before opening my mouth. Bee was standing up, apart, leaning against the sink where she'd been filling the kettle to make tea. ~And some personnel in common, I added. Bee put the kettle on the hob, but didn't turn it on. I thought her movements were unusually deliberate, exaggerated, as if directed at an audience in the cheap seats far away. When she judged the moment right, she said: It's fucking Easton, isn't it? And – it was, although I wasn't going to say so, not with the look on Bee's face, but also: not only him. She said: You should go to the police. Did she mean me, or JJ? Either way, it would be madness. She said: You weren't involved with them – she must mean JJ? – so you go to the police, you tell them everything you know, everything about Easton, and Simpson and anyone else. JJ, moving just as slowly, just as deliberately as Bee had, swallowed his whisky and placed the empty glass back on the table before he said: Why would I do that? Bee looked as if she couldn't understand what he was saying, so JJ continued: I wasn't involved. Like you said. ~You said. ~Like *you* said, he repeated, but this time he was looking at me. ~So why should I go to the police, Charlie? Which was a reasonable question. I said: No reason, I wouldn't. ~You wouldn't? ~If I were you. Which I *could have been*, but ~You *should*, Bee said. Because, if you don't, I will, and – *can you imagine that, Diana?* Can

143

you imagine what must have been going on in your aunt's head to threaten her own husband? – *Perhaps not. Perhaps I should ask Frances?* – I said I thought that would not be wise, and Bee said she was well past caring what I thought, which I didn't respond to, other than to let it hang in the air between us long enough to dry. I said we shouldn't do anything silly. Wilmots had plenty of work that was nothing to do with JJ; JJ had plenty of contracts out that were nothing to do with Wilmots. So what we had to do – *all* we had to do – was keep our heads down and go about our business. ~Your business, Bee said. ~Our business, I replied, and she said:

~JJ's not in business. You took that choice.

Through all of which, JJ stared at his empty glass, re-filled his glass, drank his whisky and stared at his empty glass again, as if we weren't talking about him. Perhaps we weren't. Rome is called Rome because, when they were about to build it, Romulus killed his twin Remus in a fight over which hill to build it on. Ten minutes, that's all it took, the difference between him and me.

Bee sat down, finally, never having made the tea, and reached towards JJ. I thought she was going to grab his glass, but instead she laid her hand on his wrist. She held it lightly and said: You're not a criminal, JJ. You're a man doing his best, and ~*Seven people died*, he said. Three of them here. In this flat. ~But you didn't kill them. ~You said I should resign. ~Because I thought you should. I thought we should get away from here. But I was wrong, and – if she was expecting some reaction here, some contradiction, she didn't get it – you were stronger than me, she said. You were right. You rebuilt the place. You put things right. You have nothing to fear.

There was a longer silence still until I said: And the rest of us?

Bee sighed. ~I don't care, Charlie. If you're bent, you can take your chances. ~If I'm what? ~Oh, come on, you know what I meant. ~No, Bee. Spit it out. But she chose not to recognize the threat in my little innuendo. ~You're a crook, Charlie. JJ isn't perfect, but he's not a crook. You get what you deserve. I couldn't let her do this, so I said: Like you? ~What about me? ~I got you. That stopped her. Now she knew the collateral damage would not be only and exclusively other people. I was hoping Rochester was right, Diana, that men – and women: he didn't say women, but that's what I was hoping – do the right thing only out of fear. That we'd all be cowards if we durst. *She'd dared once.* Ten minutes, I could have been JJ, he could have been me – but, before Bee could reply, JJ looked up and said: There are photographs.

I'd been thinking the same thing, of course, because there *were* photographs: pictures of nightclubs, politicians, developers and architects and brown envelopes and JJ, hand outstretched, or a man indistinguishable from JJ, in a suit like JJ's, in JJ's suit. I knew that, but how did he? Had Brian shown him the photos? I couldn't imagine it. Cllr Easton? It seemed unlikely. Peter? *Philip?* Between Bee and me, I thought, JJ hadn't taken much persuading, really, that the Rochester refurbishment should be gold-plated, and that Wilmots were the right people for the job.

~People died.

Bee went to the police anyway – at least, she said she did – but how much she could tell them that they didn't already know is hard to say. Philip pleaded ignorance when I pushed him. But when, a fortnight after our conversation in the kitchen at Bee and JJ's flat – *the Williams' flat: Beth and Gwyneth and David's flat* – when the police arrested Cllrs Easton and Simpson, they came for JJ, too. Absurdly, all three were kept in overnight – there was talk of manslaughter charges – and in the morning Cllr Simpson was found hanged in his cell: he'd used his shirt sleeve for a noose.

Peter Sack arranged bail for the other two.

◊

WHAT HAD BEE been up to, JJ, while we were playing farm boys in the Herefordshire countryside? Hanging around South Ken, getting under her father's feet as he, after a decade of semi-retirement, found himself newly occupied with deliciously hush-hush stuff at the Admiralty? Hardly. Packed off like a crate of cabbages to the middle of nowhere with a label tied through her buttonhole? Yeah, right. She'd have been seven or eight when the bombs started falling, a couple of years younger than us, but that wasn't the real difference, was it JJ?

Bee spent the war with "Lady" Antonia and her grandparents at the family place in Norfolk, which it would be an exaggeration to call an ancestral pile, she insisted later, when such things were an embarrassment. It was the largest house in a small village, all the same, the kind of house where once a week the local bobby cycled over from the next village to check that everything was all right, and was given tea and biscuits in the kitchen by the housekeeper, or crumpets in winter. She liked her grandparents, Bee told us, and they liked her, too. If her mother resented her exile from the city, or chaffed at having to live once more with her own parents, she didn't let it show. Which is what breeding is for, I suppose, or used to be. Her trips up to town, at least in the early years of the war, were few, and short. Bee's father could look after himself. She was happy to be in the

147

country. And Bee was happy too. She enjoyed herself, enjoyed the war

who didn't?

That's right. It wasn't you who cried yourself to sleep at night, and cried every morning. You enjoyed it too, all right, enjoyed the motorbike, enjoyed Hope, even enjoyed working on the farm. Getting up in the dark to slither through mud and shit never bothered you. Nothing bothered you then, did it? There were jobs to be done and you would do them. You wouldn't have minded fighting, if the war had gone on long enough. There were Germans to kill? You'd kill them. Cities to bomb? You'd bomb them. Houses to build? You'd build them. Stoicism? Duty? Idealism? I've known you all my life, JJ – setting aside the first ten minutes, when I wasn't really concentrating anyway – and even I don't know. I've known you all your life. Your whole life, beginning to end – *it's not supposed to work that way.*

I hated it: the war, farming, Herefordshire, Hope – I didn't hate Hope. You couldn't, really, no one could. And the boy at the neighbouring farm – *I can't remember his name* – I couldn't have hated him. I can remember Prime Ministers back to Lord Salisbury, but I can't remember that, because – honestly? – Prime Ministers are a click away on Wikipedia and, for all the wonders of the information superhighway, it can't yet answer the really tough questions like: *who was the boy I tried and failed to fall in love with back in 1944, and is he dead yet?* I bet he is. And – yes, Diana, I know we don't call it the information superhighway any more. I'm old, I'm not stupid. I know you can't hate all of something. Anything. We don't have it in us.

All the same, when we got back to London, to Peckham, I had no desire to up sticks again, no desire to breathe the clean country air of bloody Bromley, and was not at all sorry when Tony's obstinacy and laziness thwarted Angela's ambition at every turn. Not sorry that we stayed. We wandered the bombsites together, JJ and me, trying to avoid the gangs of boys about our age staking out their territory with knives and razors. Inevitably, we had our run-ins, our narrow escapes and escapades with which I could regale the congregation in the morning – what do you think, Diana? But we managed to keep our noses clean, if occasionally bloody. We got stuck into school, both of us, which was a bit of a turn up, after four years where school had been little more than a place to keep dry between farming chores and mucking about in the barn with Hope. We won scholarships, and left Angela gobsmacked at the thought of Jellicoes – our kind of Jellicoes, not your first Earl Jellicoes – at university! We'd be Bachelors of Arts, with Honours! And that would be just the start of it, wouldn't it? You have to train longer than the degree itself to be an architect, and I, I was never sure I could really draw – I could add up but I couldn't draw – so *we didn't*, but you did. And that's where we parted company, you and I, where we diverged – *no longer identical* – because I heeded the call of the National Service Act, while you deferred. I spent three months in RAF Hednesford and eighteen in Malaya, which they always say – *who says?* – was at least a clean war, compared to some, but was it bollocks –

Kenya was no better

I never said it was, but nobody wants to hear that *Chips With Everything* cobblers now, do they? No one's interested now because – *we were lucky* – we both came home alive and neither of us had to kill communists, not with our bare hands. You were fine, and I – I'd spent three months on boats, there and back again, with nothing but books and a couple of hundred bored young men for company, and *we were not the same.*

It's getting light. The window behind my work table faces west, faces the remaining darkness, but already I can make out the cigar-tube bodies of the first jet liners, not just the winking lights, as they start their long descent into Heathrow. The polling stations open in a couple of hours. I have not yet begun, much less finished, my eulogy – your eulogy – and the racket of the birds is already dying. It must have been about this time that Cllr Simpson – this time of night, of the morning, the time you know there's no more chance of sleep, and you are going to have to face the brute fact of yet another fucking day – about this time when he decided, with some relief, I dare say, that he simply couldn't. I've no idea if his remand cell had a window. I imagine not, but in any case the sky would not have been lightening then, in the foothills of winter, the way it is now, in June, almost midsummer, but it makes no difference. The insomnia would have been no more bearable, the coming day no less implacable, for the lack of light.

What are we to make of it, another day?

Cllr Easton was composed of sterner stuff. He conducted a vigorous defence, and received his sentence with dignity and charm. It was only corruption, after all – the manslaughter charges having melted away before his former colleague's corpse had cooled. He would emerge unscathed a few years later, I believe, to an active retirement on the Essex coast.

JJ wasn't put to that test. I dare say he would have been steadfast under interrogation, but – *as we gather here to remember* – you all know the next bit, I'm sure. And if you don't – if it isn't part of your family history, the tales you tell at Christmas and birthdays – you'll have seen it coming all the same. In a speech, half the trick is luring people to the point where they already know what you're about to tell them, and can congratulate themselves on being clever enough to have seen it coming, so here goes:

JJ was not prosecuted, let alone imprisoned, because, after the fun of making Bee beg me to do something I was always going to do anyway – I'm not perfect, but I'm not evil – and following a chat with one of Peter Sack's lawyers, I, Charlie Jellicoe, stepped forward to help the police with their enquiries.

~This man in the photograph, the one in the ill-cut suit? Yes, my client can confirm that's him, detective. ~No, he wouldn't say his employers are in the habit of paying him in cash, in nightclubs. But is there any law against it? ~Indeed. And if you check my client's tax return for the financial year 1966/67, you will find it there, included in the category of bonuses for exceptional performance.

They checked, of course, and there it was: £300, on which income tax of three shillings and eight pence in the pound was duly paid. Was that really all? £300 was worth a lot more in those pre-devaluation, pre-OPEC-crisis days, but even so. Was that really all the envelope contained? No, not really. You want the truth for once, Diana? The truth was that the envelope contained nothing more than cut up strips of that morning's *Daily Telegraph*. I couldn't tell them that, though, could I? They'd never have believed me.

No, I'm not perfect. But I'm not bad either.

So I kept out of Rochester House, out of Bee and JJ's kitchen for a while after that because even though she should have been grateful, they should both have been grateful – because I'd put myself in the line of fire for JJ, hadn't I? – I guessed they might not see it that way, and – *truth be told* – I didn't want to see the fall-out between them, either. Bee had said JJ wasn't a crook, and technically he wasn't. But technically, neither was I. Which didn't mean she wasn't . . . disappointed. She'd married an idealist she now thought had feet of clay. She'd wanted him to resign when Rochester House collapsed, and she'd only ever half-believed the redemption myth I'd been spinning to keep him pinned to his job. She'd campaigned for more and more money to be spent on the refurbishment and now it looked as though she'd just greased the wheels of our corruption. So, no, I wasn't going to be her favourite brother-in-law, whatever else she might hold against me. But what had JJ done? *Bugger all, that's what*. Nothing but sign the contract. Which didn't make him innocent in her eyes, let alone heroic, now. It made him complicit. Pusillanimous. Spineless. Guilty by omission and association, and not the man she thought she'd married. And what did that make her? Angry, was my guess. Guilty, too, in her own eyes, but she would batten that down until it burst out as rage. So, no, there were definitely better places for me to be that winter than the eighteenth floor of Rochester House.

Northampton, for example, which had a Development Corporation and was officially a New Town – despite being nothing of the sort – where houses were now sprawling across green fields like an army on manoeuvres. It was as pleasantly mediocre a place as any in which to keep my head down. It also had a nightclub in what passed for the louche end of town that did theme nights, transmogrifying every twenty-four hours from Northern Soul to biker gang to prog rock to – unbelievably – screaming disco queen, but that's another story. I couldn't hide out there forever. JJ's council had a new Leader, and, over lunch in Northampton's only French bistro (*moules frites* and Baked Alaska their specialities) Peter Sack suggested it would be in my best interests, as much as those of my employer, if were I to meet him.

What else could I do? I was only forty-three. I couldn't give up now.

When I returned to London, things at Rochester House were even worse than I'd anticipated. ~Where's Bee? I asked cautiously when JJ turned from the front door and drifted, barefoot, not into the kitchen but the living room. The flat had a dense, musty smell I'd never noticed there before. ~Where's Bee? I said again as I sat in the armchair opposite JJ. I'd lived in enough digs in enough Midlands towns to recognize the scent of tinned Fray Bentos scorched in an over-hot oven. ~Congreve House, said JJ. ~Oh, right. She'll be back soon, then? You could see Congreve House from the window of JJ's living room, from the sofa he sat in. He snorted, shook his head, but said nothing. ~How have you been? I said, thinking it had been years since I'd put to the test the old theory that close friends and family can be just as comfortable in silence. Bee had always filled any vacuum Nature might otherwise have abhorred. He shook his head again. ~She's with Suzanne Cluny, he said. ~Who? ~Bee, you moron. I waited. ~Suzanne is an artist, he said, eventually, spitting out the word the way he might have said 'fascist' or 'pederast'. ~She paints vaginas, he added, with her own menstrual blood. I laughed. I assumed that he and Bee had been fighting, and that laughter, a bit of male bonding – not my usual forte – was what he was looking for. ~I mean it, he said. ~Well, you have to admire her resourcefulness. He snorted again. I tried again: How about you? How's work? ~She's not just popped over for a cup of tea, Charlie. ~No? ~She's living there. ~In Congreve House? ~With Suzanne Cluny. The acid in his voice would have dissolved teeth. I'd never heard him speak like that of anyone. ~Right, I said, knowing *Really?* wouldn't help. But *really?* Bee? I suppose I shouldn't have been shocked, but I was, and then I was amused, tickled pink, you might say, although obviously I didn't. Not to JJ. I may not be the most tactful twin a brother ever had, but I'm not an oaf.

Should this be the period in JJ's life I focus on, tomorrow – the decade in which he knuckled down and got on with stuff?

Money got tight and the building boom dried up until 1979, when everything fell off a cliff. Managing 40,000 homes was still a job for JJ, though, a job for anyone: a job worth doing. Running a department, committees in the evening, tenant consultations at weekends: he made himself available. Living alone, though, that was a job too. Personally, I'd never done anything else, but for JJ it was work. Coming home, trying not to see problems on the estate – it's hard not to notice the piss-filled lift has broken down again when you live on the eighteenth floor – eating leftover meals from whenever he'd last cooked, having a drink – just a drink, maybe two: not *having a drink* the way Angela had a drink – and watching the lights go off in Congreve House. He'd go to bed and read reports, and fall asleep with papers spread across the double bed. He'd wake up to find them scattered on the floor, and he never once complained, not to me and not, I honestly believe, to anyone else. When I asked him how he was, whether I wanted to know or was merely being polite – which, because he was never angry, I had to be, more and more, despite him being my brother, my twin, despite all that – he'd say: I'm all right. A bit tired, maybe. And when he said it, what did he mean? He meant he was all right. Getting on with the job. Dedication has its place, I suppose, but it doesn't make for lively anecdote. And he was nothing if not dedicated. A lot happened in that decade: the European referendum that we lost, the long, hot summer of '76, the IMF crisis – *What crisis?* – the Silver Jubilee and its idiot twin, punk – *Say something shocking!* – the winter of discontent, Thatcher, riots, Right to Buy. But I'm writing a eulogy, a panegyric, not a history lesson. JJ was all right. A little tired. His marriage had collapsed: he'd have been entitled to a touch of self-pity if hard work hadn't been more his style – and who's to say he wasn't right?

I was all right, too, or at least in the same neighbourhood. With Peter's help, Brian and I just about kept Wilmots afloat through the second half of the 70s, clinging on to contacts in the hope of better things to come. Cllr Welland, for example, Cllr Easton's successor, to whom JJ was not keen to introduce me. Beyond not keen: whenever I alluded to the possibility he conspicuously ignored me and I did not push the point. There were other ways. Welland was an outsider, parachuted in by Labour's NEC to damp down any residual scandal, and he needed allies. Our access – Peter's access – to the Party hierarchy was more important than JJ's relationship with his own Leader. Cordial relations were established between Wilmots and Cllr Welland, and dozens like him – councillors and ministers and builders and architects and planners and union leaders. There is nothing in a Quantity Surveyor's training that equips you to calculate the value of such relationships, but they were far more important for Wilmots' survival into the feeding frenzy of the 1980s than my familiarity with the fluctuating price of cement. I was not short of things to do. I was all right, I *was in the prime of life*, and – Georges came and went.

And Bee? I'd say she flourished. Sometimes I'd ask JJ if he knew how she was getting on. He'd never answer directly, but he'd talk about the tenants association she was chairing now, how it was becoming more strident in its criticisms of the Council. ~Strident? He said he didn't mean that, and, for what it's worth, I don't think he did, not in the bitter, sexist way he might have done. He didn't think she was going to turn a south London tenants association into a lesbian-separatist collective (though she did get the Rochester declared a Nuclear Free Zone). But he had to admit – at any rate, he admitted – there was justice in her complaints, the tenants' complaints. We'd tied the panels back together, no more had popped out and plummeted to earth, no one had been decapitated by falling masonry or watched their loved ones slide out of their living rooms into the blue empyrean, but all the same the concrete had started to decay, the joints to rust, there were poisonous shit-brown stains on the outside walls and ineradicable damp within. ~I blame the builders, I said. ~So do I, said JJ. I waited for the laugh, but it never came. ~So what are you going to do about it? ~What can we do? There's no money. ~You could knock it down and start again. ~There's no money.

That's what he said, but it wasn't true. There is always money: even if for the moment it was hiding.

So we approached our fiftieth birthday simultaneously – what was ten minutes after half a century? – but separately: me, after a few years of belt-tightening had sharpened both my hunger and physique, in the very prime of life, more or less; JJ looking like a man coasting towards death. *Too much*, Diana? I don't know. Working hard, I'll give you that. Doing the right thing. But was it any *fun*?

Was it Angela who arranged the family party, who said we might have forgotten *her* fiftieth, but she wouldn't let her baby brothers pass such a landmark without a celebration? Was it?

Unlikely, given that somewhere between Watergate and the Birmingham pub bombs her liver had finally waved a curdled yellow flag in the face of overwhelming firepower. By the time 1981 rolled around, JJ, she'd been dead for years. Goodbye. She'd had some fun. She must have, somewhere down the line.

Some seasons in the sun?

Indeed. Terry Jacks. God-awful shit. And it turns out, it's not that hard after all to die – not for Angela, and not for you. For me, maybe. And no, I don't imagine for one moment she hummed that twaddle on her deathbed. It might have been all over the place at the time, but hospital radio generally takes a dim, censorious view of maudlin ballads about death. Still, every time I heard it – and on building sites in those days, you heard it quite a lot – I couldn't help thinking: at least she's been spared this, the lucky cow. It truly is an ill wind that blows no one any good.

It must have been you, then, Diana, who organized it. Unless it was Frances – *it wouldn't have been Frances* – I'm pretty sure it wasn't me. I know I'd remember having written round the family, debating with myself, however fleetingly, the wisdom of inviting Bee. And it sure as hell wouldn't have been *you*, would it JJ, who hired a hall and haggled with the caterers over sausage rolls and *vol-au-vents* – there were *vol-au-vents*, I'm sure; and not just because this was 1981 – who shipped in red wine and white wine and Campari and soft drinks and case after case of canned Heineken? It wouldn't have been you because by then, thirteen years after the collapse, seven years after Bee left and Angela died, five years before you would retire – *we're getting there, I promise* – you did nothing, did you? Nothing but work. *There's nothing wrong with work*, you said. *It's how I make the world a better place. Remember that?* Nothing wrong, but let's face it – you'd never exactly been the life and soul of any party, had you? Not my Party, obviously. But not our parties, Jellicoe parties, either. Now – then, as we approached our combined century, as the country fell apart around us, unemployment rocketed and industry imploded and the Government taught us how to survive a nuclear war, as Brixton rose up and Toxteth burned for weeks on end and *Chariots of Fire* reminded us all just how fucking wonderful the British ruling classes were – *The British are coming!* As if that was what the world needed – through all that you went to work, you did your job, you coped, you were all right, you sold off flats because you had no choice, you jacked up rents because you had no choice, you limited the damage because that was what you could do, all you could do, the only thing you could do, and you came home and ate and smoked and read committee papers and stared out at Congreve House, like a prisoner watching a songbird on a branch outside his cell, and even Heineken could not reach the parts that held you there.

So, no, there's nothing wrong with work, but we'd agreed – hadn't we, JJ? – we didn't want a fuss, a party, people – not even family. Agreed we'd have a night of it ourselves? Just the two of us, up west. It might even have been your idea, I'll give you that. A few drinks, a meal and home for you and maybe, maybe not for me – the night would still be young even if we were getting old. At your suggestion, I honestly believe, we met early in the Admiral Duncan. You wouldn't come as far as Chelsea but were happy to meet me half way, you said. Sitting side-by-side, identical, to all appearances two queens, like the Tate's Cholmondley Ladies but with pints of European lager in place of swaddled babies, we attracted the kind of lustfully perverse attention we had only to expect in the circumstances, and which you had the grace to find amusing. We exchanged gifts: you gave me 101 *Uses of a Dead Cat* and I gave you a Charles and Diana commemorative plate, on which the heir to the throne placed his hand upon the shoulder of his future estranged wife in what appeared to be some kind of Vulcan death grip. You re-wrapped the plate and packed it carefully into your briefcase, while I found the cartoon book would just squeeze into my jacket pocket and felt relieved that Tomas would never know. ~Happy Birthday, I said, raising my glass. You tapped your glass against mine then swallowed its contents. ~It's all downhill from here, you said, and winked – winked! ~Relax and enjoy the ride, I said. So how did we get from there, a cosy corner in a crowded, noisy pub, surrounded by men in suits, men in jeans and smart casual shirts and too-tight dresses, men in leather and chains and Freddie Mercury moustaches, tall men, short men, thin men, fat men, beautiful men and downright ugly men, all kinds of men and a handful of women, how did we get from there to the back of a cab heading down the Old Kent Road?

Frances – it *was* Frances; I still blame Diana, but it was Frances who found us and told us we had to follow her. It was Frances, because if it had been Diana, we never would have moved. Diana, for all her faults, isn't stupid. She'd sent her little sister, her uncles' favourite niece while she got on with laying out the peanuts and the paper plates and – how did Diana know where to send her, JJ? You told her, didn't you? Was it idle conversation, a passing remark? Or was it insurance, like mountain climbers leaving behind details of their route: *If I don't make it out of the queer morass by ten o'clock, send the hetero-rescue team?* I don't think so, I – Oh, God, it *was* you, wasn't it? At the time, I thought your reaction to Frances' teasing was genuine. I thought the puzzled look on your face when the taxi turned onto St Mary's – we surely weren't heading for what remained of Dennett's Road? – must have been identical to my own. I thought if you had known, Hope would never have been there. I thought so, but now I think I may have been wrong all along. About you. *I may have been wrong.* After all, I thought I had no desire to return to the scene of my youth, yet here I am, now, this minute, living in the very spot where once I hung back behind a pillar, watching the dance, until an older boy led me out and taught me not to care. A boy who would have been a middle-aged man by then, by 1981: married or not married, out or not out, healthy, successful, bereaved, ordinarily dis-contented, grief-stricken, riddled with a disease we none of us knew existed, then, who might have been called George and might or might not have been there. Why would I want to put myself through that?

Frances paid off the cab and led us through the open gates, across the cracked asphalt and round to the old main entrance where she ordered us to close our eyes and – but only because it was Frances – we did. I did; I can't really speak for JJ now – *a few hours before I'll have to* – and she told me to hold out my left hand, JJ his right. She took each in hers and led us, like some Biblical parable, across the threshold, up the stairs, and back into the vaulted glass Centre, back into the Experiment I thought we'd left four decades earlier, and

SURPRISE!!!!!!!!

Is there any word more chilling on your loved ones' lips?

As if being fifty were not bad enough. I left opening my eyes as long as I decently could – perhaps if I stayed blind and held my breath long enough it would all go away?

HAPPY BIRTHDAY!!!

Frances squeezed my hand and kissed my cheek. I opened

my eyes and there they all were, crammed together in the summer evening sunshine that poured through the Centre's glass roof and glass walls, leaving nowhere to hide. There was Diana, centre stage, arms out, like Christ officiating at an over-populated Last Supper; there was Philip, Flying Squad Phil, with little Dougie, fourteen now and already taller than his dad; and there were fifty, eighty, a hundred people I didn't know. I suppose people are a necessary – if insufficient – condition for a party, and it was a family party, so the family was there in such force as our little platoon could muster. We Jellicoes are a select band, however, not much given to procreation or, until recently at least, longevity. With Mum and Dad and Angela all gone I was, at fifty, already the eldest, if only by ten minutes – the *pater familias*, if you will, although there wouldn't be much fathering going on – and half a dozen people doesn't really constitute a party. Diana – you and Diana – had drummed up a few cousins on Dad's side I'd never seen before. Along the way, the nostalgia bug must have bitten deep because later, after a small sweet sherry or two, she told us all about how hard it had been, persuading the Centre to dig out old membership records, tracking down the families who still lived locally, tracing some further afield, to Croydon and Essex and Kent and Canada and even southern Spain where the trail allowed, writing letter after letter inviting anyone and everyone she could to what had become not a birthday party but a reunion. Somehow – with your help, I realize now – she'd even found the Joneses, and though Faith couldn't make it, Hope did – a large, pasty-faced woman with hands like shovels who detached herself from the crowd and waded across the space between us as if carrying a heavy sack upon her shoulders. She wrapped me in a powerful hug and bellowed in my ear: Remember me, JJ?

You'd been right, JJ, earlier, in the pub: it was all downhill from there.

I wet my gums with brandy once again, slam down the lid of the laptop, the way Dougie told me not to. There's no ignoring the fucking daylight now. It is six-thirty, and the sad fact is that it is not unusual for me to be awake. But today there's an election. Radio 4 will kick off one of those strange days of foreign news and human interest stories, in which the ban on reporting domestic politics seems to turn the clock back decades, imposing a gentler, less combative tone in which you half expect to hear presenters read out listeners' letters claiming the first cuckoos in spring. Outside, meanwhile, London has already shrugged off its sleep and geared up for a fight that might break out at any moment, but might not: that's just the way it is, mate. The noise of airliners passing overhead is barely distinguishable from the traffic, the trains, the sirens and the background pulse of barely suppressed rage that constitutes life in this city. By the end of today, Theresa May will be PM again and you will be a small jar of grit and ash, waiting to be scattered across Peckham Rye, and could either of us really say we'd wish it were the other way around? She looks like she hates every minute of it, and who can blame her? But what did you do, JJ? You put things right, didn't you? You stuck it out, you didn't walk away – *until you did* – for five years after our surprise party, like the thirteen years before them, like every day since the first of June, 1968, you went to work each morning, you stayed at work till late, to make things better, yes, as you had for twenty years before that, but also to *make it better*, to make amends for what you'd done

we'd done

and not done, and – you made it right, every day, until long after the world had forgotten, and even the council decided it was time to give up, to move on, to tear the whole thing down and start again. Tear it down. Not just Rochester House, the whole estate.

It was Peter Sack's idea, originally, a year or two after our fiftieth. Peter Sack who suggested to Cllr Welland that the estate could be "regenerated" and, even though it wasn't the first time I'd heard the word, it still had quote marks hanging around its ears. I tried it out myself, at Peter's suggestion. JJ was not impressed. ~It's a housing estate, he said, not a bloody Time Lord. ~A what? ~You know: Doctor Who. I did, of course. In those days the Doctor was an insipid bloke in a cricket jumper who'd been a TV vet before, but you didn't actually need to watch telly to know that. ~Is that what you do, I said, when you're not at work? We were in a pub at the time – in Soho again, but not the Admiral, I remember that. ~It's one thing I do, he said. ~Interesting. ~Compared to what? Which wasn't such a bad question: what, after all, did I do with my own free time that gave me the right to patronize my brother? ~I mean, he continued after sipping on his lager for effect, I suppose I *could* spend my evenings in a chilly hall arguing about the Alternative Economic Strategy with a bunch of unreconstructed Stalinists. ~You could, I said. ~Or picking up young men on Hampstead Heath. ~I wouldn't recommend it. ~You wouldn't? He looked me in the eye until I turned away. I didn't argue the point, preferring to let this line of conversation die of its own poison. JJ was my brother, my twin, and it was not unreasonable for me to wonder what he did with his time, to worry that it was simply nothing. Watching children's TV might be better than staring out of the window at Congreve House wondering what Bee was up to, when she was coming back, but it wasn't my business – my real business, not as a brother, but as Charlie Jellicoe, QS, bag carrier, facilitator, deal-broker and, lately, partner at Wilmots Development. I had a job to do. ~We knock it down, I said, which shouldn't be that hard. ~That's not funny. ~No? Okay. We rebuild. Traditional methods. Brick – brick facing, anyway. Gardens – not huge, I admit, but they're gardens, more than they have now. ~They've got a park now, and a playground. ~They've got a dog's toilet full of broken swings. JJ shook his head: Privet hedges? An Englishman's home is his castle? ~Defensible space, JJ. Encourages people to look after the place, designs out crime. ~Yeah, yeah, blah-di-blah. It's a community, Charlie. Public space, public housing. You're pushing the enclosures all over again. ~Enclosures? What did he think this was, the Civil War? I said: We wouldn't be driving anyone away. ~But, if you knock down the towers, Charlie, they can't all fit in the space. ~Yes, they *can*. That's the point: low rise, but still high density. ~Seven hundred houses? JJ was scornful, as I knew he'd be. It was why we were having this conversation in a pub. ~Seven-fifty. We've already done the massing. Like I said, traditional methods: two, three-storey townhouses. ~Townhouses? ~Terraces. That's what they call them now. ~The old ways are the best, eh, comrade? ~Just so. ~Back-to-back? ~Of course not. I told you, JJ: gardens. ~Running water? Toilets? ~Of course, toilets. Don't be silly. All mod cons. ~*All mod cons?* How old are you, Charlie? I laughed, and he laughed. Not real laughs, of course, though I hoped mine at least looked like one. Was he relaxing? ~I don't know, JJ. What does it say on our passports? ~It says you're old enough to buy me another pint.

The pub was tiny, the bar a Victorian mahogany-and-bev-elled-glass affair I couldn't get to through three rows of drink-ers, but the staff were well trained and by the time I'd elbowed my way up, there were two pints waiting for me. When I returned to our table, JJ said: So who's paying for all this? ~The beer? ~The houses. Was he interested after all? I said, We are. ~We the people? ~We, Wilmots. He left a pause before replying, as if underlining the implausibility of what I'd just said. ~We don't pay you? Isn't that the way it works? ~Not a penny, JJ. That's the beauty of it. ~Because? ~Because you haven't got any money, have you? But he wasn't *that* relaxed. He said: Why don't we pay? ~You give us the land, we build the houses; we sell some on the market and the rest to a housing association. ~And we lose the stock? ~You're going to lose it anyway: right-to-buy has got you stuffed. ~So we just give up? I risked a sigh. ~You get nomination rights, you put your tenants and your homeless families into the housing association properties and they don't get the right to buy. ~And Wilmots? ~Gets a warm glow of satisfaction. ~Yeah, right. ~Okay, we flog the private units and that's what pays for the whole thing. Everybody wins. ~And you make a profit. ~Yes, we make a profit. Twenty percent. Industry standard. It doesn't happen otherwise, JJ. We're borrowing the capital, we're managing the project, building the houses, doing the sales. All you have to do is give us the estate. ~And let you knock it down?

This was it. There was no point in beating around the bush now.

~Yes.

JJ didn't blink. ~No.

~Everybody wins, JJ.

~Over my dead body. Which was ironic, I suppose, given how things turned out, although his wasn't the body in question.

He wouldn't budge, I knew that. When he said no, he

meant no; but I tried, all the same. Those people he was worried about, I said – his tenants, his neighbours, Bee – were living with the damp and the rot and the crumbling concrete that couldn't last much longer, and the lifts that kept breaking down. JJ said: Whose fault is that? Who built the place? ~We built it, JJ. You and me and Wilmots. Are you going to live in a dump forever just because that's the way we built it? ~I'm not in the business of selling houses. ~Oh, but you are, whether you like it or not. It's called right-to-buy. So you've got a choice, haven't you? You can let the Government stuff you, you can sit and be a victim, while all the people who pay your salary live in a shit hole till you retire. Or you can use the market to get them somewhere decent to live.

Did I believe all this? Who knows? The point was that JJ didn't, he was having none of it, as I'd known he wouldn't. For JJ something could be right, or wrong. And this was wrong. For me, things were easier. I was just doing my job, the way he did his. He rolled out all the clichés: selling off the family silver, enclosing the commons, even the Highland clearances got a mention. There has to be another way, he said. ~Or another man, I said. We'd go over his head if we had to, we'd talk direct to Cllr Welland. Peter was already setting it up. I'd hoped to get JJ on side first, but never really believed I would. If I didn't, I didn't. It made no difference.

~It's your funeral, I said.

Cllr Welland was a different story: a man of vision, Peter said. But he said it in the councillor's presence – in Welland's office, at the Town Hall – so it's not entirely obvious he wasn't just being polite. When Welland replaced the incarcerated Cllr Easton, he had not only relegated JJ and his paperwork to the second floor – where he could be *closer to his people*

- but had also thrown out the curtains and painted over the panelling in a shade of yellow that JJ said reminded him of milk that had been left too long on the doorstep. Personally, I rather liked it. With the same new broom, Cllr Welland swept out the meeting table and its armoured chairs, along with all the occasional tables and extraneous desks that had somehow cluttered up the corners of the room. In their place he installed a suite of low-slung leather sofas assembled in a rough horseshoe around a glass-and-steel coffee table that was always just too far out of reach for comfort. It was on these sofas, our knees almost level with our ears, that we sat - Peter, Brian and I - letting our coffee go cold in its bone china cups, as Peter and Cllr Welland exchanged a few pleasantries about Labour acquaintances and their manoeuvrings now that Michael Foot had resigned. Labour wouldn't win the next election, Peter agreed, but the one after that was anybody's guess. The SDP would die a painful death. ~I'll drink to that, Welland said. And so to business.

Peter deferred to Brian, who made the pitch I'd made to JJ earlier. The councillor listened without interrupting and then turned to his Director of Housing. What do you think, Joe? ~You know my thoughts, Leader.

I tried to catch JJ's eye - only Dad ever called him Joe - but he was staring resolutely at a point somewhere between us all. There had come a time, the week before, when I'd been trying to persuade him, and everything else had failed, a moment when I asked why he did what he did, why he bothered with it all, when somehow, I still don't know how, he had mentioned Bee, and I said, Bee? Is she your yardstick, even now? He said something about her chairing the tenants association, how she would have to be on board, but we both knew that wasn't what he'd meant. I said: She isn't coming back, you know. He pretended not to know what I meant, and I said: *She blew me once, did I ever tell you that?*

I shouldn't have, I know. But what can you do?

The Leader waved JJ's words aside. I know your politics, he said, but I'm the politician here. What I want to know from you is: would it work? ~That depends on what you mean. ~For God's sake. In its own terms, man. Do the numbers stack up? JJ continued to stare at the middle of the coffee table. Eventually, he said: Probably.

~Then we'll do it.

And that was that – except, it wasn't, was it? The Leader's say-so was all very well, but it would be another three years, give or take, before we actually got on site to blow the fuckers up. Three years of consultation, design, tendering, planning permission, legal challenges – thanks, Bee, for such dedication to gumming up the works – selection of preferred bidder – Wilmots, thank Christ, after all that work – due diligence, contract award, final design work, protests, Bee haranguing the planning committee, the housing committee, railing against the transfer of council stock to private developers for profit – as if it wasn't being transferred every day – decant preparations, and then, just then, when we're so strung out that just one thing, one little thing, could make us all snap, just when we're ready to go, hit

//   *PAUSE*   //

and slam on the brakes for – what? *Local elections!* As if they'd make any difference, as if there was any chance – there was no chance, surely? – that here, in southeast London, after seven years of the most unpopular government in living memory, simply not a chance that Labour wouldn't walk it? But I had long ago learned not to tell politicians to stop worrying about elections. I wasn't the one who had to knock

168

on doors begging strangers to let me keep my job, after all. So what did I know?

I shouldn't have told you that, I know, I – know that what I'm trying not to say by talking about thirty year-old elections is that I shouldn't have told you about Bee, about Bee and me, about that night, the christening party for Rochester House. I shouldn't have told you but I did, and *what I'm trying not to say is that I'm sorry.* Not sorry it happened – although I am – but sorry I told you. There was no call for that, no call.

Another drink, another brandy, the real stuff. Take the edge off all the bruising. There are holes in my trousers and my jacket where I hit the road, but I'll change. I'll have to wear the black suit later, anyway. Not much later. There's time for one more before the polls open. I have to make it – to be able to make it – there and back before Diana arrives to collect me. Voting's what we do, you did, since we were twenty-one, key to the door: since Eden trounced Attlee. Ten? Did she say ten? It's only up the road at the community centre, in the church. St Mary's: nondescript modern with grass on the flat roof at the front that isn't meant to be there – it's not one of those turf roofs, whatever Mrs. Vega says the priest says, just builder's rubble under a tattered plastic mesh that's given sufficient purchase for the hardier fescues to take root – and not one among the faithful seems devout enough to shin up there and clear the space, for Jesus' sake. It isn't far. Not far from here, I mean: it's too far for me to climb, at my age and besides, it's not my church. A couple of hundred yards, perhaps, once you're out of the gates, no need even for the Easy Rider, just the Rollator, ten minutes or so there, once I'm out of the gates, ten minutes back, fifteen at most, even in my injured state, a couple of hundred yards. There'll be no queue,

I shouldn't think, this isn't South Africa in '94, Tunisia in 2011. It isn't even the referendum last June, although it's a direct consequence of that. But this time, at least, everybody knows which way it's going to go. I'll vote anyway, I'll make my mark, even if it makes no difference. Another drink won't stop me now. How could it, when even being dead did not stop you?

In the end, whatever his misgivings, Cllr Welland and his Labour colleagues romped home. The opposition won no seats at all. They declared the Rochester Estate regeneration scheme good to go, full steam ahead, don't worry about the legals, they'll never get anywhere. We'll call the new estate the Phoenix, it'll rise out of the ashes of the Rochester, *the ashes of Robert and Catherine Peters, of Elijah Johnson, of Rabia Leel, of Beth and Gwyneth and David Williams, out of the penetrating damp and cockroach infestation, and* it was Cllr Welland himself who came up with the name this time. Neither Peter Sack nor Brian saw fit to argue. I didn't argue, either, and nor did you, JJ, you signed the contract in your own hand using, as I may have mentioned before, the fountain pen Mum gave me when we left for Herefordshire. She gave you one, too, of course, but you lost that, didn't you, or gave it to Hope – was that it? – and stole mine, I'm sure, although you never admitted it. I certainly didn't have it when we returned and went to school in London. But there it was, in your flat when you died, my pen, with which you signed, again, and, on that same day, wrote to accept the retirement package you'd agreed with the new Chief Executive and Cllr Welland. It was only right. They would top up your pension and you would retire at the earliest possible opportunity: 1st August, 1986. Our birthday: we would be fifty-five.

It's quarter past seven. Outside, the light is no longer orange, but London grey. The sound of Mrs. Vega's radio trickles faintly through the wall. On the other side – they've been here a couple of years, I don't know their names – the baby cries while the toddler is being dressed and the father looks for the fucking blue shirt he brought back from the fucking dry cleaners only yesterday, for fuck sake, and I think: serves you right. Tomas could have told you better, if he weren't dead. He must be dead, I imagine. Then again, plenty of people imagine that of me. When I heard you'd died, when Diana rang to confirm what I already knew, I said: At least no one will mistake me for him now. That's what I said, but I was wrong. At our age I *thought you were dead* is a more common salutation than the young would ever believe.

Do you get that yet, Diana? *I thought you must be dead?* Do you know anyone apart from me?

The polls are open, the great democratic process under-way once more and Theresa May, with all the charm and personality of cold porridge in which someone has stubbed out a cigarette, will no doubt be confirmed as Prime Minister, heir to an increasingly degenerate line: May, Cameron, Brown, Blair, Major, Thatcher, Callaghan, Wilson, Heath – still got it! There's nothing wrong with me. Nothing. I am older – was older – will always be older, now.

Harold Wilson died in 1995, and even though every-one had forgotten he was still alive, the bigwigs all turned out. Alec Douglas-Home died a month later, and nobody noticed. When Thatcher died, we gathered outside the Ritzy in Brixton, chanting *Maggie, Maggie, Maggie! Dead! Dead! Dead!* I can't claim it was my finest moment.

I –

I haven't slept, just a few minutes with my face on the table. Which isn't all that unusual, not now. It never was. Brandy or tea? Tea. Toast. Let's make pretend it's breakfast time. It is breakfast time. Let's make pretend I've risen, refreshed but hungry after a respectable eight hours of uninterrupted sleep and restoration.

Can I remember how that feels? When I was still employed, I used to think it was the work itself that slapped me awake, sweating, heart pounding, formless anxiety scrabbling for purchase among the flotsam of my day. If there were anyone in the bed beside me I would want to be cuddled, to be soothed, to be reassured that there was something right in my life and, at the same time, I'd push him away to shield myself from the heat of another's body, and also, if I'm honest – if I cared – to stop him seeing me like that, stop him having to hold onto my sodden pyjamas or my slick-wet flesh, to hear my guts rumble or feel the foul breath of my boiling farts against his groin as he lay spooned around me. If I cared, I couldn't allow that. I'd lie there, writing a report, a letter, rehearsing a presentation in my mind, endlessly circling around words and phrases, finding answers in the sudden clarity of three a.m., seeing they were good, that I didn't have to worry, then worrying I'd forget. I'd get up quietly if I were not alone, slip into my dressing gown – this dressing gown, the same one I've put on now, over my clothes – and feel for my glasses in the dark, feel for my slippers with my feet, and try not to let George know. I'd make my way to the kitchen and sit listening to the heavy ticking of the clock, cradling the emptiness of the insomniac while I wrote the letter, the skeleton argument, the checklist, or sketched the plan, while I got it all out of my system and chewed antacids and sipped milk, or brandy, to calm my roiling guts. After that I'd read a novel, or poetry – Rochester, perhaps – anything to take my mind elsewhere for half an hour before creeping back to bed, sloughing off my dressing gown into a silken puddle on the floor and sliding silently between the sheets to lie, prone, my hands placed lightly together on my chest like the figures on the tombs of mediaeval saints. I'd count my breaths and try not to think – and fail – and count my breaths, and fail, until, eventually, my heart would slow and I'd subside into a state just below consciousness before waking again, able to tell I'd been asleep at all only because the images I was resisting were so improbable they must surely have been dreams. In the days that followed nights like these, my chest would feel empty, my breath constricted, and I would know that I was going to die.

It was different for JJ. He had already failed, he said; and now he's dead.

I imagined it would stop, when I stopped work. Perhaps it would have been different if I'd retired properly, with a leaving do, like JJ, with speeches and cards, unwanted gifts and all the paraphernalia of a wake? I couldn't imagine it, though. Couldn't imagine one day working and, the next day – not. It seemed ridiculous to me. We were fifty-five, you can't just stop at fifty-five, can you? Apparently you could. *You* could, but – I didn't. I never really retired, just drifted out of the habit of work, a little less each year, a little more jazz and gin, a little more time for the family, some of which – most of which – I could have done without. I was all right. I still didn't always sleep at night. Anxiety never dies, it just adapts its diet, finds new flesh to gnaw on in the wee small hours. Frances, for example – a constant source of worry to a caring uncle: what was she doing now that Philip, too, had retired? Was she happy? And Frances' kid, Dougie, a boy after my own heart, or some such organ (have I already said that?) Was he? And HIV/AIDS and the cracks in the wall. Living here in the

173

Centre that isn't the Centre any more, and what that means and what that says, and you, JJ. You.

I was all right, but you? What were you *doing* for thirty years?

You *withdrew*. You cultivated your metaphorical garden; but, in the end, it was not enough. Perhaps it was never enough. We'd meet up, later - more recently, in this century that neither of us expected to see. I'd given up myself by then, given up work. But austerity bit deep - not for you, you'd never really be poor again, but for those around you, on the Phoenix Estate - and brought you back out in the end, into the food bank, the last refuge, with your bags of cereals and tinned food, and into the company of that woman you mentioned the last time we met. I don't count all that. Deathbed conversion is for Catholics, not socialists. You *stopped*. In 1986 you stopped, and I carried on. When the choice was between right and wrong and there was only wrong, perhaps that was no choice at all? Perhaps withdrawal - refusing to choose - was the only thing to do. Perhaps I was wrong and you were right, and that's what I can't say, tomorrow, because I was all right. Just a little tired.

I am all right, but I'm here, at my writing table in yesterday's clothes wrapped around with the Japanese silk dressing gown I stole from - *let's say from George, that'll do* - with a tumbler of cognac in one hand and my fountain pen, again, in the other. I think, after all, it's better that I write notes for tomorrow, for today. I'll need notes. There's no time now, no time left, to learn my lines, to do without a script, whatever Diana says, no time to memorize the words I haven't written yet, haven't finished - haven't slept, that's why I'm awake when JJ, who killed eight people that we know of never lost a night's sleep in his life, and -

174

Is that it?

It's not. The deaths were not the point, not really, and when you said you didn't want a leaving do, you surely must have known they'd never let you get away with that? You'd been there thirty years, Director almost twenty. They weren't going to let you slink away with your tail between your legs. They couldn't: what would that have said about them?

She rang me up - your PA, Janet. You remember Janet? Of course you do - *of course you don't: you're dead* - Janet worried about you, you must have known that. She'd grown middle-aged working for you. You'd asked about her weekends, on a Monday morning, asked about her children, her husband, over the years, you'd remembered their names. When she rang, she said: Does he mean it? ~He thinks so. ~Really? ~But that isn't the point, I said. Leaving dos are like funerals, they're not for the one leaving. ~So I should organize it anyway?

Why did she ask me, of all people? Because she knew me, because I'd been in your office - your old, vast office, now the Leader's office; and your smaller office, too - I'd been there on and off and was there more than ever, then, with the Rochester regeneration scheme; because I always made friends with my clients' secretaries, asking about their weekends, too, remembering what they liked to do; because I was your brother and she was afraid of getting it wrong. *It wasn't Janet's idea* to combine the demolition ceremony and the leaving do.

We had to put it back a month to coincide with your last day, the day before our birthday. I had to lie and tell you I was sorry there were glitches, we were revising the project plan, I couldn't tell you the exact date, yet. Normally you'd never have put up with that, but you were leaving. You said we'd have to talk to the housing committee chair, who'd want to push the button. And, normally, you'd have done that yourself. But you

175

were leaving, things would happen after you left, after you, they would keep happening and you knew that.

You didn't know I'd already spoken to Cllr Simpson – *not Cllr Simpson, he was dead, hanged in a prison cell in 1974* – spoken to the new chairman, whatever his name was, persuaded him to share the limelight. It will come, the name – *44 minus 7 equals 37, minus 7 equals 30.* Nothing wrong. You didn't know, when you left your office at lunchtime on the day before our fifty-fifth birthday, before your retirement started, when you strolled along the corridor to the Council chamber, where you expected, against your expressed desire, to be met by your colleagues for a buffet of sandwiches and sausages on sticks and slices of bubble-gum pink pork pie, you didn't know that you'd find me, and only me – SURPRISE! – and that I'd escort you out to the town hall car park and insist you get into my car – not the TR3 by then, the Citroen DS I bought after seeing one in that French film we all raved about in the early 80's, remember? *Of course you don't remember,* but it doesn't matter. You said: Where are we going? ~All will be revealed. You weren't happy, that much was obvious, but, as I'd told Janet, that really wasn't the point. ~Don't be difficult, I said. A lot of people have put a lot of effort into this. You slumped low in the passenger seat, your head barely above the dashboard, as if trying to make yourself disappear. ~You never could resist the call of duty, could you? Except, he was leaving. Withdrawing.

We pulled out into the midday traffic in silence. I switched on the radio and the mother of a missing estate agent appealed for anyone who knew anything about her daughter's disappearance – until JJ leaned forward to retune the radio. Lugubrious choral music filled the empty spaces of the car, insulating us against the summer sunshine with a darkness all its own.

When it became obvious where we were going, he said: Oh, God. ~He won't help, I said. You don't believe. ~Oh, God. ~Come on, I said. It'll be fun. ~Fun? ~Round things off with a bang. *Which, obviously, I've often wished I hadn't said, but*

When we pulled into the estate there was no disguising the scale of the preparations. The Rochester was broadly elliptical, an elongated clock face in which the four towers were placed at twelve and two and four and six, with a low-rise chain of maisonettes that snaked around the later hours from six to midnight. In the once-green space between them, as far from Rochester House itself as it was possible to arrange, and separated from the rest of the estate by temporary metal fencing, a newly-erected marquee was thronged with people. There were a couple of hundred at least: employees and former residents, local journalists and catering staff hired to run a makeshift canteen and bar. Up on the flat roof of the low-rise immediately in front of the marquee, and visible to those within it, was a temporary stage, complete with a lectern and microphone and a trestle table on which there sat a polished wooden box. Wires trailed from the box to join those from the microphone and speakers, bundled and taped securely to the roof. We did not want the Chief Exec or Cllr Berger – *that* was his name, the housing chair who wasn't Cllr Simpson – didn't want either of them, or the Leader, tripping and falling from the roof. Or JJ, of course.

~Oh, God. ~Stop that, I said. You'll love it, really. I parked the car. We got out and walked towards the marquee, shading our eyes from the sun. Janet spotted us and hurried over. She hugged JJ who stood rigidly, his arms held out at his sides, as if to avoid untoward human contact. ~I'm sorry, she said, not letting go, and – gradually – JJ's arms relaxed into a brief embrace. Janet stepped back. ~I'm sorry, she said again, but she was smiling. I know what you said, but . . . we couldn't just let you go . . .

By now others had spotted our arrival. They were trailing over from the marquee, plastic cups of wine or beer in their hands, paper plates of chicken curry, dhal and rice. Those with free hands tried to shake JJ's, the others just nodded their greetings – congratulations, they said, all the best – sorry to see you go – thanks for everything – what are you going to do? – lucky bastard! – you're too young to retire! – *what . . . ?* – thanks, boss – don't go! – all the best – *what on earth?* – see you – *what . . . ?* – lucky bugger – what are you drinking? – *what ARE you going to do?* – but you shrugged them off, shaking hands where it couldn't be avoided, muttering thanks, wishing colleagues well, avoiding the questions – *the* question, the only question – until someone handed you a pint and you sipped it gingerly, as if suspecting it was poisoned, as if nothing had changed since we were fourteen, since the night the Centre re-opened, the Experiment re-started, then swigged more eagerly, as if you thought it didn't matter anyway.

Janet, pointing towards the bar, said Cllr Berger is already here, the Leader, too. We're just waiting for Roger. The new Chief Exec was called Roger Farley, and looked it: tall, broad-faced, sandy-haired and none too bright, as if he should be teaching rugger at a minor public school. Which just went to show. I liked him. After the nod from the Leader, it was Roger's energy that was going to bring Rochester House down again after all these years, Roger who had driven the deal from their end. He knew what he wanted.

JJ hung back, not keen to plunge into the marquee, where the benedictions and the questions – *the* question – would have come thicker and faster than ever. We waited by Dryden

House while Janet went to find the councillors. The entry phone had been battered in and the metal security grilles over the doors and ground floor windows papered over with crude anarchist posters. All around the block, in a continuous thread like crime-scene tape, they'd spray-painted FUCK OFF YUPPIES . . . YUPPIES FUCK OFF . . . FUCK OFF YUPPIES . . . YUPPIES FUCK OFF . . .

I said: You have to hand it to them. JJ didn't answer, so I read one of the posters. ~Look at this, I said. It was a cartoon of two men, one short and fat, the other impossibly thin, both decked out in waistcoats, monocles and top hats. *We say fuck off to pink gin-swilling refugees from Toffsville.* Still JJ said nothing. ~It's like *The Beano* with Tourette's, I said. ~They've got a point, he said. ~They have *not* got a point, JJ. We're building social housing here. ~You're building a few cheap houses – and some fucking expensive ones. ~That pay for the rest, I said. I wasn't going to debate whether the council owning them was the point, not on JJ's last day, not when it wasn't like we hadn't had the conversation once or twice or a thousand times before – no matter – *Thatcher, Callaghan, Wilson, Heath . . . 23, 16, 9, 2 . . . that's right, I think.* I was spared JJ's attempt to pick a fight by Roger Farley, who approached us with his hand outstretched, his face pink and shiny in the summer sunshine, a dark, damp patch on his shirt only partly covered by a broad orange tie. ~JJ! Congratulations! He nodded to me. ~Charlie. I nodded back and pointed at the wall behind us. ~We've been enjoying the redecoration. He ignored that. ~Is Cllr Berger here? JJ said he was, and the Leader. ~Janet's gone to wrangle them out of the bar. ~The Leader? You are honoured. JJ didn't answer. I said: He's been here thirty years. ~Man and boy, said Roger.

The Leader hadn't, though, had he? Cllr Welland. He'd

not been here in '68, when Rochester House collapsed; or '72, when we put it back up. By the time he moved to London the tenants were already complaining about the leaks and broken lifts, but there he was, and there we were, and Roger and Cllr Berger. We must have been a strange sight, the five of us, plus Janet hovering like an anxious stage manager, on the roof with the makeshift sound system. Like the Beatles on the Apple offices, Frances said, afterwards, later, when it was all over. ~JJ Lennon, I said, playing along. ~Minus the sideburns and the fur coat. ~Roger would have to be Ringo, I said. ~So was the Leader Paul? she said. JJ and I both laughed, in his case probably for the first time since that day, the day it happened: Cllr Welland was about five foot four and nearly as wide. ~Of course, JJ said, the Walrus was Paul, and - *that was more like it*. ~So who were you, Frances asked me. ~Me? Billy Preston. ~Who? ~The session man they brought in to hold it all to- gether. Because like the Beatles - *not like the Beatles* - we'd trooped up onto the roof, squeezing one by one through an access hatch, JJ and I treading warily across the flat asphalt, knowing just how flimsy it could be. ~Best keep to the edges, Leader, JJ said, as Cllr Berger approached the microphone and tapped it experimentally, producing a series of dull thuds like coffins knocking together in a mortuary. ~Good afternoon, he said, but the hubbub from the marquee below continued unabated. He hit the microphone harder, repeatedly. ~*Good afternoon!* he bellowed, and his voice bounced back to us from the walls of Rochester House opposite. People began to file out into the space between us and the marquee, most of them holding drinks in one hand, raising the other to shade their eyes as they stared up, and - whoever set this up had clearly not taken into account the position of the sun - they looked as if they were saluting, like some alcoholic passing out parade.

~*Ladies and gentlemen*, the chairman of the housing committee continued, peering a little nervously down at the crowd
below. He was a councillor of the old school, an electrician
with decades of public speaking behind him, but still more
at home in a poorly-attended committee room. ~*Colleagues.
Fellow residents* – he had once lived on the estate himself, and
wasn't going to let us forget it – *today is a very special day*.
I estimated that, from where they stood, with their angle of
view, most of the crowd could perhaps see Cllr Berger from
the knees up, Roger, JJ and me from the waist, and the Leader
– who was not only shorter than the rest of us but was unchar-
acteristically holding back, allowing his deputy to bask in such
limelight as the occasion afforded – must have appeared as no
more than a shrunken head perched on the parapet wall. ~*A
very special day*, Cllr Berger repeated, his words rebounding
lazily from wall to wall in the heavy summer air. *It is both the
end of an era and the beginning of a bright new dawn.* I was
watching JJ now: his eyes were closed. ~*And Jolyon Jellicoe* –
there were a couple of sniggers in the crowd at that – *Jolyon
Jellicoe has been both a faithful servant and a guiding light of
this council's housing department for longer than most of you
can remember. Indeed* – he held up one finger – *for longer
than it has been this council* – please God, I thought, don't
let him get sidetracked onto the Borough mergers of 1965;
but he paused, resisting the temptation with palpable effort,
before going back further still. ~*In 1954*, he boomed, *when
Jolyon joined us, all this* – he gestured broadly towards the
empty tower blocks, the boarded-up maisonettes, the barren,
grass-free space cracked by the hot, dry weather – *all this was
nothing but slums. Real slums, condemned since the war as unfit
for human habitation – those that hadn't been bombed out – but
still packed with people. People like my family . . .*

I tuned out, knowing he'd get back to JJ in the end, but it might take a while. A few of the council employees were getting bored, too, drifting surreptitiously back into the marquee, or spreading out to find shadier spots between the blocks. A couple of women hovered at the fence, then pushed past the temporary barrier and disappeared from view. I wondered where Bee might be: she surely wouldn't be here? She had campaigned hard against the redevelopment, and lost. She would have hated all this. I didn't enjoy the thought, but there it was.

~ *in a very real sense,* Cllr Berger was saying, *it is those lives, as much as the bricks and mortar, that will be forever Jolyon – JJ's – legacy –* wait: which lives? But he was already moving on to the future – *a future of decent, modern homes, built in partnership, managed in partnership with the local community,* he said, pausing instinctively for the anti-gentrification heckle that never came. This wasn't a tough crowd, after all: they were mostly on the payroll, and only those residents who'd campaigned in favour had been invited. (Although, now I thought about it, one of the women slipping through the barrier had looked a lot like Bee.) We were all here to smooth over the cracks. Even JJ. It was his last day, but the retirement do he didn't want was providing one last service to the administration.

Cllr Berger finally ceded the microphone, inviting JJ to say a few words. He stepped forward, but was deftly intercepted by Roger Farley, who thought it only appropriate, he said, standing sideways to the mike and looking across the roof at JJ, that he add his thanks and congratulations to Joe on behalf of all the staff. Which was fine, of course, and part of the plan, but Roger was a Chief Exec and couldn't help talking about himself as well. ~*I can't claim to have worked here since Harold Wilson was in short trousers*, he said, turning towards the audience, and waiting for the sympathetic laugh. *In 1954 I was swotting away in school* – he shook his head and grinned – *I always was a bit of a duffer. In 1954,* he repeated, *when Joe Jellicoe* – *JJ to many of you* – *arrived to start work here as a fresh-faced trainee architect, Winston Churchill was still Prime Minister, we were just celebrating the end of rationing* – *enjoy your curry!* – *and Roger Bannister was running a four-minute mile. Across the country, we were building 250,000 homes a year. And* – he paused, gazing out at the towers around us – *many of those homes were here, in the skies of south London. Many being built by men* – *and women* – *like Joe Jellicoe, men and women who knew that the people living in damp dark crowded slums, whole families to a room, with no indoor toilets, no hot water, were still people, with hopes and dreams* – *and rights* – *like everybody else, and* – that's where he was wrong, where he would always be wrong: to be similar is precisely not to be identical. JJ wasn't like the people he housed, however long he held onto his tenancy: he had once *been* one of them – we both had – but not now. We were different people now – *and if mistakes were made*, Roger said, dropping his voice and moving closer to the microphone, *whatever mistakes were made* – Behind the crowd, behind the marquee, a couple of floors down from the top of Rochester House, a window opened, then another. White sheets began to unfurl. Somebody was inside the tower. I turned to JJ. There was nothing in his face. Roger Farley kept talking, either too myopic to see the banners that now covered the outside of two floors, or pretending that he hadn't, perhaps, hoping to keep everyone looking his way. *But time moves on*, he said. *We grow up, we grow old. Our ideas and our buildings grow old, too. The Rochester was this council's first high-rise estate* – it wasn't, but no one was going to correct him – *so it is only fitting that it be re-born as our first estate regeneration, in partnership with the best of the private sector, and that Jolyon Jellicoe, who did so much to create this, this* – he gestured to the towers, the boarded-up convenience store, the swing-less playground – *this* community, *to nurture and support it through troubled times, only fitting that, before he leaves us, on this, his last day of thirty-two years' service, that he should be the one to set its resurrection in motion.*

He turned to beckon JJ forward, leading the applause himself. In blood-red lettering I realized later was probably actual blood, the banners he'd been ignoring read: SAVE COUNCIL HOUSING – SAY NO TO PRIVATE PROFIT – SAY NO TO THE PHOENIX. Two women – one of them definitely Bee – emerged at the foot of the tower, scrambled across the empty playground, over the barrier, through the clapping crowd and into the block we stood on.

JJ approached the microphone cautiously, as if uncertain of its purpose. He closed his eyes again, waiting for the applause to die down. ~*I was going to say a few words, too. Mostly I was going to say thanks.* He paused. Behind him, behind us, Bee emerged through the hatch onto the roof, followed by the second woman who must surely have been Suzanne Cluny. ~*But after all that,* he said, gesturing towards Cllr Berger and Roger Farley, *perhaps I'd better just get on with it.* He stepped briskly across to the trestle table with the wooden box and slammed his fist down on the big red button. There was a deafening boom, the kind that turns your bowels liquid. The crowd turned as one to see a rabble of pigeons fleeing Rochester House, then – nothing.

~It's just to scare the birds, a voice said from below as a patter of what sounded more like small arms fire triggered clouds of dust around the tower's skirts. Smaller clouds puffed through the upper storey windows and Rochester House began to collapse in upon itself, floor after floor disappearing into the billowing pall, the banners quickly swallowed up. There was another heavy crump, and a chunk of masonry the size of a Ford Fiesta blew out and up above the estate, describing a perfect parabola over the temporary fence, over the marquee, over the crowd's upturned faces – as it began its descent I could just make out the orange and brown striped wallpaper you had put up before Bee left – over the parapet wall it came, lower and lower, over JJ, over me, over the Leader of the Council and down to land, with horrific predictability, on Suzanne Cluny, and, with her, to crash straight through the flimsy asphalt roof, through the bedroom below and into the kitchen below that. And, when the grumbling roar of flying debris finally ended there was a moment of pure, shocking, terrifying silence before the screams began.

◊

I HAVE DRUNK two cups of strong black coffee and swallowed a handful of ProPlus. I have been to vote. I walked – despite the growing pain in my right knee and elbow, and the dull ache in my head – not much more slowly than usual, to the polling station. There wasn't much of a queue. My fellow citizens were not, at this still early hour, flocking to St Mary's to fulfil their democratic duty. Of the three poll clerks, two looked bored already – perhaps, having performed the same task twice in the last two years, they were merely resigned to a long, slow day – but the third, a young man with a pencil-thin moustache and a rather natty two-tone suit of the sort I had last worn in the 1960's, took my polling card and read the number to his colleague as if it were the last communiqué from General Gordon, an allusion which no doubt would have been entirely lost on him. His colleague flipped a page or two, ran a finger down the list and then, with the aid of a biro and a metal rule, scratched out my name. The final clerk in the line-up passed across a ballot paper and pointed me towards the booths as if, in this otherwise empty hall, I could possibly have missed them. I duly manoeuvred my Rollator across the stained parquet, took the soft-leaded pencil and, once I had shaken its tether out of the way, wrote in fat black letters across all of the candidates' names and all of the boxes:

Robert Peters
Catherine Peters

Elijah Johnson
Rabia Leel
Beth Williams
Gwyneth Williams
David Williams.
I paused for a moment, and then added:
Suzanne Cluny.
I folded the paper and, after slowing re-crossing the floor, dropped it into the black tin ballot box. For the first time in my adult life I had not cast a valid vote. It would make no difference, I knew, least of all to those who died. Their names would be read by no one but a weary election teller. It would do no good. And yet, you had already voted. It was the least that I could do. I doubt I'll get another chance.

Diana will be here again soon. I shouldn't complain. None of it is her fault, and she is only trying to help.

It could have been me – I know that now.

There was nothing inevitable about it. When that car-sized block of your old flat crashed into the low-rise, it could have been me between it and the asphalt roof. It could have been you. It could have been Cllr Welland or Bee, but above all, it could have – perhaps should have – been me. But the universe is not moral and history has no arc. Its trajectory is an irregular spiral, turning constantly in upon itself, like a tangled skein of wool. If there is an end, a destination beyond mere annihilation, it is lost to sight. You can trace Prime Ministers back – back before we were born, JJ, back through Lloyd George and Asquith and Campbell-Bannerman, back into the dukes and earls – although no Jellicoes – right back to Robert Walpole, Earl of Oxford, the first Prime Minister as such, until the line disappears in a morass of Chancellors and lords high treasurer – but you can't trace them forwards. Listen to me, losing it. *I'm not losing it*: how many sevens are there in a hundred? Fourteen and a bit. There's two left over and what happens when you take away another seven? You get to *minus 5, minus 12, minus 19*, because numbers aren't people, you can keep depleting them, there is no end to it. That's what negative numbers are for: so you can keep going back, going lower, and lower, deeper and deeper down and there can be no fucking end to it and perhaps that's what I should say, this morning, at the Honor Oak Cemetery and Crematorium?

My brother is dead, not me.

After the demolition, after you withdrew, we did not speak for a decade. Not deliberately, at least not on my part: there was no great rift between us. No anger. Or no more than usual. I don't imagine you attended Suzanne Cluny's funeral; I certainly didn't think it was my place. If you were called to the coroner's inquest it was not on the days when I was there. The coroner blamed the negligence of a sub-contractor. Wilmots survived, again. We rebuilt the estate. You did not attend the topping-out ceremony, though I know you were invited.

You simply stopped. Stopped working, stopped coming to family get-togethers, stopped calling. You disappeared, as if you were dead. Not as if you were dead – I am your brother, I would have known. I heard you had been decanted to a flat out by the motorway. It sounded pretty grim, but I never visited. I heard you moved back into the estate, the Phoenix, when the rebuilding was complete. Penance? Is that what it was?

I heard Bee moved to Hackney, somewhere off the Kingsland Road. I even met her once, in a gallery in some newly fashionable corner of Shoreditch. I was there for work, and we went for coffee. She'd given up teaching for a campaign job, for some cause or other. She had met somebody new. She would always be grateful to Suzanne; she would always love JJ; she was happy. I didn't believe a word of it. I told her I was happy too, and we kissed each other's cheeks, and after that I heard nothing more for years. When you went into hospital, I had Dougie google her. She's back in Norfolk now, with three dogs, a wife and a relaxed attitude to the privacy settings on her Facebook account. They look content with their lives, although the recent posts seem to be almost entirely about Brexit and Donald Trump. She is not in favour. Dougie messaged her, but there was no reply. When JJ died, he sent the details for tomorrow - today - but I don't suppose we'll see her there.

Would you, JJ? If she'd died first?

Would you?

She never was my wife.

I carried on. The Phoenix Estate - and subsequent contracts we won off the back of it - kept Wilmots busy. Then I realized it had been almost a decade, and that it was ridiculous. We were going to be sixty-five. If you hadn't already retired, you'd be about to retire. What *were* we doing?

I called, but the number I had no longer worked. I drove to the Phoenix and asked after you. I dare say there would have been an easier way - I still had contacts in the housing department, after all - but, having decided at last to track you down, the idea of working the streets like a superannuated private eye appealed to me. I even wore a homburg, one of those I'd mothballed in 1959. I knocked on doors. I stopped people in culs-de-sac where as many front gardens boasted mature privet hedges as cars with aerodynamic spoilers made from kits. I raised my hat, pointed to my face and asked if anyone knew a man who looked like me. For a long time no one admitted it, whether out of circumspection in dealing with an apparent lunatic, a natural inclination to withhold information from nosey strangers, or genuine ignorance I will never know. Eventually an old woman – that is, a middle-aged woman younger than us, but who contrived to look like older women looked when we were young – replied, when I asked again, if she knew a man who looked like me: *Are you all right, Joe?* I explained I was not Joe, I was his twin, looking for Joe, whose address I did not know. ~Of course you are, dear. I asked her to tell me where you lived. ~You want to know where you live? I said yes, because it was easier. We were only sixty-five: surely not old enough to be that confused? I played along.

She led me lightly by the arm a hundred yards or so along the street before parking me at the front door of a tiny brick-faced house with arrow slits for windows. ~Will you be all right? I thanked her and said I would be fine. I rang the doorbell while she stood by watching me, obviously uncertain if she should leave. ~Have you lost your keys? When, eventually, you opened the door, she exploded in nervous laughter. ~Pauline? you said. ~Sorry, she said, still laughing in the face of the apocalypse, He said he was you. You smiled. ~Hello, Charlie. Why would you do that?

After that, we called each other up from time to time, met every few months. He would never come here, to the Centre, but was still happy to meet in Soho, even though it was no longer mid-way, or convenient for either of us, or even really Soho any more. The writers, artists, musicians and drunks had all long gone. Old Compton Street was a gay theme park. The GIRL with the handwritten MESSAGE sign had been evicted from the flat above the members' bar I used to drink in; the members' bar had become a coffee shop. You'd never minded being seen out on the streets with me. Not even when being me was against the law. Which was big of you, I have to say – *you big old straight bear* – even if you preferred the professional me, the suit and tie pitching to the board me, the deal on the golf course me, although you never could stand golf and hated the idea of deals being done anywhere but an office in the presence of a lawyer and an accountant, sealed and signed – *with a stolen pen* – or maybe you didn't. Maybe you really didn't care. You always were a better man than I ever gave you credit for.

So there we were, early one spring evening a few years later, at the fag end of the century, so to speak, looking for all the world like a couple of old queens: sad and a bit baggy but still game. Even if you weren't, we were two men together: me dressed up for a Friday night at the Admiral, you my still closeted friend. The tourists cutting through to Shaftesbury Avenue would have had to look harder now to see we were identical: not scene clones, not just brothers, in fact, but twins. Identical. Except not. Nothing like.

You stupid bastard, what are you doing dead?

But there we were, at the end of April, 1999 – believe me, I've not forgotten the date – sauntering towards the pub, when it exploded, and – *this is not a metaphor.*

The pub exploded.

It was a warm evening and already – this early in the evening, this early in the year – drinkers in shirtsleeves were standing outside on the pavement when the window disintegrated, spraying shards of glass through their lightly-clothed flesh.

And there it was again: the silence.

We've all become familiar with the soundtrack of atrocity. It has three stages, beginning with the blast you feel as much as hear – in your chest, in your guts – the depthless bass that crushes the breath from your lungs and opens up the ground beneath your feet; it ends with screaming, with ululation and, eventually, sirens and the diminuendo of professional jargon and radio static; but in between, for a moment that stretches implausibly, impossibly from split seconds into whole lifetimes, there is silence. The actors move in slow motion, their mouths agape, bellowing soundlessly while the star searches frantically for the child/lover/colleague they're supposed to protect from all harm and we are reminded that this is fiction, that in reality we cannot save the ones we love and they will not save us. The silence is not a metaphor, either: it is real.

The explosion was real. The silence was real. In time, the screaming would be real, too, but in the moment of noiseless fear on Old Compton Street I recalled the warnings, because we had been warned. There had been posters urging vigilance. It was – briefly – like the 70s, like the war, like July 2005, like Manchester a fortnight ago and London last weekend. We are warned every day, now – but what can we do? Bombs fall out of the sky like concrete. Life goes on. It isn't heroism, isn't even stoicism. Or commitment. It's just brute fact. Life goes on and there's not a fucking thing that we can do about it.

That's why Mum and Dad are dead and Angela is dead, and now you're dead, JJ, and I'm not.

Not because you are a worse – or better – man. Not because you were right, and maybe I was wrong. That with-drawal was better than complicity. And not because the good die young – we're eighty-five, for pity's sake – but just: because.

And that's why in – what? – two hours from now, as Bach or the Beach Boys fade away, I'll haul myself up and stagger unaided – *I don't need any help* – to the pulpit, to the lectern – *it's not a fucking church* – with these notes in my left hand, my stick – *my knobkerrie* – grasped firmly in my right, and I will say a few words about my brother, my twin, the man I have never, not once, saved, in eighty-five years.

A mirror image is not identical: it is the exact opposite.

I know that now. I could not have been you.

I reach for my Rochester, for the battered paperback Bee gave me half a century ago. I flip through its creased and annotated pages, certain now that I will find something absolutely, perfectly – *really* – inappropriate to say.

Forgive me, JJ. It will be fun.

ACKNOWLEDGEMENTS

ALL BOOKS ARE built out of countless other books. Here are some of those that really helped me build this one:

Being Me and Also Us: Lessons from the Peckham Experiment, Alison Stallibrass, Scottish Academic Press, 1989

Concretopia – A journey around the rebuilding of postwar Britain, John Grindrod, Old Street Publishing, 2013

Collapse: Why Buildings Fall Down, Philip Wearne, Channel 4 Books, 1999

Estates – An Intimate History, Lynsey Hanley, Granta, 2017

The Five Giants: A Biography of the Welfare State, 3rd ed. Nicholas Timmins, William Collins, 2017

Modernity Britain 1957–62, David Kynaston, Bloomsbury, 2013

When the Lights Went Out: Britain in the Seventies, Andy Beckett, Faber & Faber, 2009

Promised You A Miracle: Why 1980–82 Made Modern Britain, Andy Beckett, Allen Lane, 2015

State of Emergency: Britain 1970–74, Dominic Sandbrook, Allen Lane, 2010

Seasons in the Sun: The Battle for Britain, 1974–1979, Dominic Sandbrook, Allen Lane, 2012

National Service: A Generation in Uniform, 1945–1963,

Richard Vinen, Penguin, 2015

Life in 1940s London, Mike Hutton, Amberley, 2013

Radical London in the 1950s, David Mathieson, Amberley, 2016

Selected Works, John Wilmot, Earl of Rochester, ed. Frank H. Ellis, Penguin, 2004

A Room in Chelsea Square, Anonymous [Michael Nelson], Jonathan Cape, 1958

Saturday Night, Sunday Morning, Alan Sillitoe, W. H. Allen, 1958

Room at the Top, John Braine, Penguin, 1960

Mates, Tom Wakefield, Gay Men's Press, 1983

The websites of the Pioneer Health Foundation; the Royal Institute of Chartered Surveyors (RICS); the Royal Institute of British Architects (RIBA); the Socialist History Association and the Socialist Health Association also proved invaluable.

This book has been typeset by
SALT PUBLISHING LIMITED
using Neacademia, a font designed by Sergei Egorov
for the Rosetta Type Foundry in the Czech Republic. It
is manufactured using Holmen Book Cream 70gsm, a
Forest Stewardship Council™ certified paper from the
Hallsta Paper Mill in Sweden. It was printed and bound
by Clays Limited in Bungay, Suffolk, Great Britain.

CROMER
GREAT BRITAIN
MMXXII